Samuel French Acting Edition

CW01022916

Play On!

by Rick Abbot

SAMUELFRENCH.COM   SAMUELFRENCH.CO.UK

ISBN 978-0-573-61361-6

www.SamuelFrench.com
www.SamuelFrench.co.uk

FOR PRODUCTION ENQUIRIES

UNITED STATES AND CANADA
Info@SamuelFrench.com
1-866-598-8449

UNITED KINGDOM AND EUROPE
Plays@SamuelFrench.co.uk
020-7255-4302

Each title is subject to availability from Samuel French, depending upon country of performance. Please be aware that *PLAY ON!* may not be licensed by Samuel French in your territory. Professional and amateur producers should contact the nearest Samuel French office or licensing partner to verify availability.

MUSIC USE NOTE

Licensees are solely responsible for obtaining formal written permission from copyright owners to use copyrighted music in the performance of this play and are strongly cautioned to do so. If no such permission is obtained by the licensee, then the licensee must use only original music that the licensee owns and controls. Licensees are solely responsible and liable for all music clearances and shall indemnify the copyright owners of the play(s) and their licensing agent, Samuel French, against any costs, expenses, losses and liabilities arising from the use of music by licensees. Please contact the appropriate music licensing authority in your territory for the rights to any incidental music.

IMPORTANT BILLING AND CREDIT REQUIREMENTS

If you have obtained performance rights to this title, please refer to your licensing agreement for important billing and credit requirements.

CHARACTERS

(in order of appearance)

AGGIE MANVILLE – a stage manager and prompter
GERALDINE "GERRY" DUNBAR – a community theatre director
HENRY BENISH – "Lord Dudley" – a Character Actor
POLLY BENISH – "Lady Margaret" – a Character Actress
MARLA "SMITTY" SMITH – "Doris the maid" – a Supporting Player
SAUL WATSON – "Doctor Rex Forbes" – a Villain
BILLY CAREWE – "Stephen Sellers" – a Juvenile
VIOLET IMBRY – "Diana Lassiter" – an Ingénue
LOUISE PEARY – a sound and lighting and scenic technician
PHYLLIS MONTAGUE – a novice playwright in the community

SETTING

The stage of a community theatre.

TIME

The present.

ACT I

A rehearsal of Phyllis's *Murder Most Foul*.

ACT II

The dress rehearsal of their play.

ACT III

Opening night of their play.

AUTHOR'S NOTE

For simplicity's sake, the speeches in *PLAY ON!* which appear in quotation marks are speeches from *Murder Most Foul*, the show-within-the-show; all other speeches are, of course, the words of the actors in *this* play, not the play they're *doing*.

ACT I

(Curtain rises on the not-quite-furnished set of the play-within-the-play, Murder Most Foul. *It looks as pictured in the "play setting" diagram in this script, but the sofa and armchair, right now, are represented by folding chairs, three for the sofa and one for the armchair, and the upstage corridor wall is not yet in place, so that we can see the theatre wall itself through the upstage doorway, and any "backstage clutter" one might normally see in such a place – a ladder, a saw-horse, buckets of paint and brushes, etc. Other accoutrements of the set, however, are as they will appear in the play-within-the-play when it is finally given.* **PLAYERS** *in this act will wear casual rehearsal clothing.)*

(Note: A seat in the front row, in the downstage right area, should be reserved for **GERRY** *for all performances, of course.)*

(At curtain-rise, **AGGIE MANVILLE** *is onstage, watching the curtain open, warily, as a stage manager should.)*

AGGIE. *(Calls offstage.)* Okay, hold it, that's fine!

(Curtain stops, and she peers out into audience.)

Gerry? How's that?

GERRY. *(From rear of theatre.)* Where's the upstage corridor wall? Aggie, I thought I told you –

(She will walk down aisle to front edge of stage, during:)

AGGIE. It was too wobbly. They're putting on a couple more braces.

GERRY. *(Will come into our view; she is* **GERALDINE DUNBAR**, *the director; middle-aged and pleasant-looking.)* I hope they don't make 'em too bulky – our people have to be able to cross backstage *behind* that thing!

AGGIE. *(Shrugs.)* That's what I *told* them. All we need is somebody breaking a leg.

GERRY. Where are our players?

AGGIE. *(Jerks a thumb offstage.)* Going over their lines. You want 'em?

GERRY. Of course I want them! It's only three days till dress rehearsal! We've got to get this show moving!

AGGIE. *(Calls.)* Hey! Onstage, everybody!

> *(Through various doors there will wander in:* **HENRY** *and* **POLLY BENISH**, *a couple in their middle-fifties;* **MARLA "SMITTY" SMITH**, *a pretty-but-awkward girl of about seventeen;* **SAUL WATSON**, *a thin, mustachioed man of about forty-five;* **BILLY CAREWE**, *an athletic-looking young man of spirit, about twenty-five;* **VIOLET IMBRY**, *a pretty face behind which medical science may someday discover a pretty brain, about twenty-two; and* **LOUISE PEARY**, *a sad-faced woman in plaid flannel shirt and denims, carrying a roll of gaffer's tape, about thirty-five; all save* **LOUISE** *are carrying "nine by twelve" binders containing scripts for their play; the* **BENISHES** *will sit upon the sofa, the others will remain standing.*

> *(Note: For this act, "sofa" and "armchair" refer to the folding chair substitutes for these items.)*

GERRY. Louise, don't you have any work to do?

LOUISE. *(Defensively-but-pessimistically, as she nearly always speaks.)* Aggie said everybody.

AGGIE. I didn't mean you.

LOUISE. I'm somebody.

GERRY. Everybody in the *play,* Louise.

LOUISE. She shoulda said so.

> *(Exits the way she came in.)*

GERRY. Now, is everybody here?

VIOLET. Not counting Louise.

GERRY. I know, Violet, I know.

POLLY. *Can* we get *on* with the *rehearsal*?

> *(Before anyone can reply, we hear the sound of hammering from the direction in which* **LOUISE** *vanished.)*

HENRY. Does she have to do that *now*?!

GERRY. Louise!

LOUISE. *(Off. Hammering stops.)* What?

GERRY. Do you have to do that *now*?

LOUISE. *(Offstage.)* You want that corridor wall or don't you?!

GERRY. Isn't there anything *else* you can work on?!

LOUISE. *(Offstage.)* I guess.

GERRY. Good. *(Gets command of herself.)* Now, ladies and gentlemen, let us take the action from the top of Act Three. We've wasted enough time already.

POLLY. *I've* been ready for half an *hour*!

BILLY. Who *hasn't*?!

GERRY. I'm sorry I was late. We've only got the one car, and Frank had to work late –

SAUL. You should've called *me* – I go right by your place, Gerry.

SMITTY. Saul picks *me* up for *every* rehearsal.

BILLY. *(Kidding* **SAUL**.*)* Does Margie know that?

SAUL. Aw, c'mon, Billy! Can't have Smitty coming by bicycle after dark.

GERRY. People, can we have these charming conversations later? We've got to get this *show* rehearsed!

POLLY. That's what I've been saying all along! Haven't I, Henry!

HENRY. Yes, dear.

GERRY. Polly, we're all as anxious as you are. This is a first play, by a new author, and we want to do it justice.

SAUL. Justice tempered with Mercy.

POLLY. *I* happen to think it's a *lovely* play!

SAUL. Sure. You've got the fattest part!

POLLY. How dare you!

HENRY. Darling, *he* means you have the most *lines*!

POLLY. I know *very well* what he meant!

GERRY. *(A bit stridently.)* Might I remind you all that the author will *be* here at dress rehearsal – and we *still* haven't learned the third act?!

> *(All grimace, and ad-lib mumbled apologies, and start getting into position, during:)*

And what about those scripts?! We should have been off book two weeks ago!

> *(Positions for the play-within-the-play will be: **HENRY** at the sideboard, **SAUL** before the safe but facing into the room, **POLLY** in the center of the sofa, **SMITTY** just out of sight and ready to enter through stage right doorway, **VIOLET** in armchair, and **BILLY** standing just upstage of armchair.)*

> *(Note: These will always be the "top of Act Three" positions for the group.)*

BILLY. *(Tosses script onto left third of sofa.)* I know *my* lines.

POLLY. *(Drops her script atop his.)* And I know *mine*.

GERRY. How about the rest of you?

(They ad-lib apologetic mumbles, but put scripts down.)

SMITTY. *(Offstage.)* Should I come in?

GERRY. *(Moves back and sits in front row, on:)* As soon as I give the signal. All right, everybody – top of Act Three... *Curtain!*

VIOLET. "Ah, Lord Dudley, you give the most charming parties – !"

(And curtain starts to descend; **GERRY** *leaps up.)*

GERRY. *Louise!*

LOUISE. *(Off. While curtain continues to close.)* What?

GERRY. Leave the damn curtain alone!

LOUISE. *(Offstage.)* But you said –

GERRY. That was for the *players*! We're *starting* the act, not *ending* it!

(Curtain pauses wherever it is, and starts reopening.)

LOUISE. *(Offstage.)* I was only doing my job!

*(***PLAYERS** *ad-lib mumbles as curtain comes full open.)*

GERRY. That's fine! Now leave it *alone,* Louise, okay?

LOUISE. *(Offstage.)* Fine by me!

GERRY. *(Sinks into seat again.)* Okay, everybody, from the top again!

VIOLET. *(After a pause.) Now?!*

GERRY. Yes! Now!

VIOLET. *(A bit flustered.)* "Ah, Lord Dudley, you give the most charming parties in the whole of England!"

HENRY. "You are too kind, Diana. A pity Sir Percival could not be here."

POLLY. "Do you know – I'm *worried* about Percival! He's never accepted an invitation to one of our parties and then not shown up – at least, not without sending word."

(*There is a silence;* **PLAYERS** *slowly look toward* **BILLY**.)

BILLY. Oh, is that *me*?

GERRY. I thought you *knew* your *lines,* Billy?!

BILLY. I do! I just forgot where I'm supposed to say them.

POLLY. (*Stands up.*) I can't stand it! He's doing this on purpose! I know he is!

GERRY. Polly, sit down! Billy, pay attention to the cues! Take it back a line, and start again!

VIOLET. Whose line *is* it?

AGGIE. Polly's.

GERRY. (*Just realizing.*) Aggie! *Why* are you still onstage?

AGGIE. If I stay in the *wings,* I can't *hear* them!

GERRY. If you heard them, why didn't you throw Billy his line?!

AGGIE. Because you said not to throw them any lines unless they asked for them! I thought he was just pausing before speaking.

GERRY. All right, all right. Aggie, get the hell off stage!

(**AGGIE** *will turn and exit, during:*)

Everybody get back into positions. We'll take it from the top!

SMITTY. (*Offstage.*) Do *we have* to?!

GERRY. YES!

SMITTY. (*Offstage.*) You don't have to yell.

GERRY. That's what *you* think! (*Enforcing a calmness on her voice.*) Now – shall we begin once again – ?

(*All* **PLAYERS** *mumble assent.*)

Good. Take it from the top. Violet, go ahead.

VIOLET. (*Composes herself; then:*) "Ah, Lord Dudley, you give the most charming parties in the whole of England!"

HENRY. "You are too kind, Diana. A pity Sir Percival could not be here."

POLLY. "Do you know – I'm *worried* about Percival! He's never accepted an invitation not to show up at one of our parties – " I mean –

GERRY. Go on, go on, go on!

POLLY. *(Recovering.)* " – to one of our parties and then not shown up – at least, not without sending word."

BILLY. "Ah, but Lady Margaret, he might have had motor trouble."

VIOLET. "Yes, indeed. I do hope *he* hasn't had an accident – !"

GERRY. No, no, no! That's " – he hasn't had an *accident*!"

VIOLET. That's what I *said*!

GERRY. You said, " – *he* hasn't had an accident!" As if someone else *did*!

VIOLET. Should we take it from the top?

POLLY. Oh, damn it!

SMITTY. *(Offstage.)* Come *on*, Violet!

VIOLET. All right. *(Back into character.)* "...I do hope he hasn't had an accident. These roads can be treacherous at night."

SMITTY. *(Enters and curtseys to* **HENRY**.*)* "Begging your pardon, milord, but should we delay dinner any longer?"

HENRY. "Mmm – no, I think not. Can't wait for Percival forever."

> *(Moves toward* **POLLY**.*)*

"Shall we, my dear?"

POLLY. *(Rises.)* "I suppose so. But – don't you think someone should call Percival's flat and ascertain the reason for his absence?"

BILLY. *(Coming around armchair to take* **VIOLET***'s arm as she rises.)* "Do you know – that might be a sound idea. There is something distinctly odd about all of this."

VIOLET. "All of what, Billy?"

> *(All* **PLAYERS** *sag, excepting* **VIOLET**.*)*

BILLY. Violet, you did it again!

VIOLET. Did what?

BILLY. Called me by my own name! I'm "Stephen"! "Stephen Sellers"! And you are "Diana Lassiter"! Is that so hard to remember?!

GERRY. Billy, do you *mind*?!

BILLY. What – ? Oh, sorry, Gerry.

GERRY. Take it from Violet's line.

VIOLET. Okay. *(In character.)* "All of what, Stephen?"

BILLY. *(Goes to speak, goes blank, sags, calls:) Line!*

AGGIE. *(Offstage.)* "This business about Percival and – "

BILLY. *(Interrupts.)* Got it! *(In character.)* "This business about Percival and the necklace. He *did* say he was bringing it tonight, Lady Margaret?"

POLLY. "Well, actually, I never spoke with him directly – but there was a message delivered this morning in the post."

SMITTY. "What, on Saint Swithin's Day?"

HENRY. "By Jove! Never thought of that! Margaret – are you *certain* about that message?"

POLLY. "Why – come to think of it – no."

VIOLET. "You *didn't* receive a message?"

POLLY. "Oh, yes – I did – but now I wonder if it actually were from Percival!"

BILLY. "I should very much like to *see* that telegram!"

GERRY. *(Jumps up.)* No-no-no! You've jumped the lines!

BILLY. Oh! Sorry. Just a moment – yeah, now I've got it. *(In character.)* "But it did come by post?"

POLLY. "I – I assumed it had – but – "

HENRY. "Assumed? You mean, you didn't actually see it?"

POLLY. "Why, no."

VIOLET. "Then how did you know its con*tent*?"

GERRY. "*Con*tent!"

VIOLET. " – *con*tent?"

POLLY. "Why – Doctor Forbes told me what it had said."

(**PLAYERS** *look toward* **SAUL.**)

SAUL. "Is there any reason I shouldn't have?"

BILLY. "No, no, of course not, old chap. Only – if there was no delivery of the post, today, then how – ?"

SAUL. "It was not a letter. It was a telegram."

BILLY. Uh – uh –

GERRY. *Now* you say that line! The one you jumped before!

BILLY. *(Into character.)* "I should very much like to *see* that cablegram!"

AGGIE. *(Offstage.)* *"Telegram"!*

BILLY. Oh, hell, what difference does it make?!

GERRY. None! But if Saul says "telegram," then *you* say "telegram"!

SAUL. What do you mean, "if"?! I *always* say "telegram"!

POLLY. *I* don't give a hoot in hell *who* says *what*! Can't we get *on* with this disaster?!

HENRY. If we'd get *through* the thing once, we could start *polishing* our *parts*!

POLLY. And when do we get the real furniture? These metal chairs are painful to work on!

SAUL. But they help you polish your parts...?!

POLLY. *(Incensed.)* There! He's doing it again!

GERRY. Saul, will you stop with the jokes and buckle down to work?!

SAUL. I was just trying to ease the tension.

HENRY. Your jokes about Polly are *causing* the tension!

SAUL. Okay-okay, no more jokes. Now can we please get back to the play?!

(*Offstage hammering starts again.*)

GERRY. *Louise!*

(*Hammering stops.*)

LOUISE. *(Offstage.)* I thought I could get the job finished while nobody was working.

GERRY. We're about to *start* working!

LOUISE. *(Offstage.)* Well, why didn't you *say* so?!

> *(We hear clunk of dropped hammer.)*

I'm gonna make some coffee.

GERRY. *Fine! (Regains some control.)* Now – please – everybody in position, and we'll pick it up at Billy's line, all right?

> **(PLAYERS** *mumble assent; then:)*

BILLY. *(In character.)* "I should very much like to *see* that telegram!"

SAUL. "Well – as a matter of fact – I don't have it. The message was phoned from the telegraph office."

BILLY. "Doris – have there been any telephone messages this evening?"

SAUL. "See here, you insolent young pup! Are you doubting my word?!"

POLLY. "Of course he isn't, Rex! Stephen, you should apologize to Doctor Forbes."

BILLY. "Oh, I shall. As soon as Doris answers my question."

> *(As* **PLAYERS** *look toward* **SMITTY,** *there is a crash backstage.)*

POLLY. What was *that*?

AGGIE. *(Offstage.)* Louise dropped the coffee cup tray!

LOUISE. *(Offstage.)* You bumped it out of my hands!

AGGIE. *(Offstage.)* The hell I did!

GERRY. Did anything break?

LOUISE. *(Offstage.)* I don't think so.

AGGIE. *(Offstage.)* She bent one of the spoons.

LOUISE. *(Offstage.)* That *was* bent!

GERRY. Ladies! Ladies! Can you hold it down, *please*?!

> *(Listens; silence; sighs in relief.)*

Okay, let's pick it up where we left off.

SMITTY. *(In character.)* "No, sir."

BILLY. *(Wasn't ready.)* What?

SMITTY. I said –

BILLY. I *know* what you said, I just wasn't ready for it.

GERRY. Go back to Billy's line and start again.

BILLY. Okay. Um...oh. "Oh, I shall. As soon as Doris answers my question."

SMITTY. "No, sir."

POLLY. "What, are you quite sure?"

SMITTY. "The telephone has been out of order since this afternoon, *mum!*"

GERRY. Wait, wait! Smitty, that's short for "madam" – it doesn't mean the *phone* was keeping mum!

SMITTY. Oh! Oh, *I* see! *(Back into character.)* "...out of order since this *afternoon,* mum!"

BILLY. "Aha! And what do you say to *that,* Doctor Forbes?"

> (**SAUL** *opens his mouth, then pauses, frowning.*)

GERRY. Saul, that's your cue!

SAUL. Didn't we skip a page? This part is coming too early.

GERRY. Aggie – ?

AGGIE. Wait a minute, I'm trying to find the place. What page are *you* on?

GERRY. I left my script at home. I was so anxious to get the car, that as soon as Frank came in, I took right off without thinking about it.

AGGIE. *(Comes onstage, holding script.)* You know, I think Saul's right – we go right from page three-two to page three-four. Who's got a complete script?

> (**PLAYERS** *grab up their scripts, start paging through them.*)

BILLY. I've got it! Page three-three. Saul's right! We skipped the whole bit about the diamond necklace.

AGGIE. How come *I* don't have that page?

GERRY. Oh, dear, maybe I miscounted when I was getting the Xeroxes made. Does everybody *else* have it?

(PLAYERS ad-lib assent.)

GERRY. Okay, then, let's back up and do the part we skipped.

AGGIE. How can I follow along without that page?

SAUL. Here, take *my* script. I've got the lines down cold. *(A little testily.) If* I ever get the chance to *say* them!

BILLY. Say, while we're stopped, I've got a question.

GERRY. *(Wearily.) What?*

BILLY. It's about the play's title – isn't that a steal from something else? An old Agatha Christie movie, I think it was.

VIOLET. Oh, *I* don't think Phyllis Montague would *steal* a title, Billy.

SAUL. There's no way she *could*! No one can copyright a *title*! It's the law. There just aren't enough words to go around to name things.

BILLY. Even if that's true – what about the advertising for our show? Won't some people think this show *is* by Agatha Christie?

POLLY. *(Shrugs.)* So much the better for our box office!

HENRY. And it *is* a murder mystery, so no one gets hurt!

VIOLET. Doesn't sound like much of a murder mystery, if no one gets hurt...?

SMITTY. *I* thought Sir Percival got bumped off by Doctor Forbes – ?!

GERRY. *(Who has been trying to regain control of the group during the overlap-delivery of preceding eight speeches.)* Hold it! All of you! Did we come here tonight to rehearse, or to discuss Originality versus Plagiarism?

BILLY. Gerry's right. Let's get back to work. Sorry I interrupted.

POLLY. Which line do we go back to?

SMITTY. Yeah, where does the necklace come in, anyhow?

AGGIE. *(Moving offstage, reading from script.)* Oh, I see what happened. Smitty, you came in too early.

SMITTY. I did? I thought I was supposed to enter when Violet says that line about the treacherous roads.

AGGIE. *(Laughs.)* You're *almost* right – it's where she says the line about "lecherous toads!"

SMITTY. Oh, gee, I'm sorry. But it *sounds* about the same.

SAUL. Phyllis Montague fancies herself a poet.

POLLY. She *is* a poet. A rare talent – and a great writer!

SAUL. Would you say that if she had you playing a *mute*?

HENRY. Now, see here – !

GERRY. Stop it, all of you! Smitty, listen to me – this is important – you *mustn't* take your cue from the words alone. Pay attention to the *plot.* Then you'll *know* when you're supposed to enter, even if Violet says the line *wrong,* don't you see?

VIOLET. *I* didn't say the line wrong!

BILLY. You didn't say it at *all*!

VIOLET. Well, how *could* I when Smitty came in *early*?!

GERRY. All right, all right, that's enough! Do your arguing on your own time.

LOUISE. *(Offstage.) Coffee's* ready!

AGGIE. *(Closes script.)* Finally! I could *use* a cup!

POLLY. But we've barely gotten started!

GERRY. Listen, maybe a break is a good idea. Let's all have a cup, then take this thing from the top and get it right!

BILLY. *Now* you're talking!

> (**PLAYERS** *will emigrate toward sound of* **LOUISE***'s call, and* **GERRY** *will come up on stage to join* **AGGIE** *as they exit.)*

GERRY. Aggie – don't go yet. I want to talk to you. I'm getting very worried about our progress.

AGGIE. *What* progress?!

GERRY. *(Laughs ruefully.)* I know what you mean. We've never been this far behind on a show.

AGGIE. It's not your fault, Gerry. We've never had the illustrious *author* in our hair before, either! If Phyllis didn't keep *rewriting* the damned show while the cast is trying to *learn* it – !

GERRY. She's *promised* not to change anything *else*, Aggie.

AGGIE. What do you want to bet she's going to show up here with seven new pages?!

GERRY. Oh, *don't,* Aggie! *They* haven't learned the *last* batch of rewrites!

AGGIE. Small wonder, the way Polly keeps inviting Phyllis to dinner, and getting her part fattened! It's almost as big as *she* is, now!

GERRY. Aggie, don't *you* start with the fat jokes, please! I'm having enough trouble with *Saul*!

AGGIE. If Polly had her way, this play would be a one-woman *monologue*!

GERRY. Well, at least Phyllis is letting us do her play *free*!

AGGIE. Naturally! Nobody would pay *money* to do it!

GERRY. Be fair, Aggie – it's not *that* bad.

AGGIE. Oh – I suppose not. But if Polly keeps padding her part – !

GERRY. She won't. I'll have to put my foot down. Three days until dress rehearsal – we'll be lucky if we learn the lines we've *got*!

AGGIE. Oh, I don't know about that – some of the *mistakes* tonight are better than the *original* lines! If you'd just let the cast alone, this show could be a riot!

GERRY. Aggie, *Murder Most Foul* is *not* a *comedy*! Phyllis Montague would *scream* if the audience started *laughing* at it! She'd pass right out on the floor!

AGGIE. Well, then, you'd better have the smelling salts handy for opening night.

GERRY. Oh, Aggie – !

> *(But before they can continue,* **PLAYERS** *start returning to the stage, sipping coffee, so they let it drop.)*

GERRY. *(Starts off.)* Is there anything left in the pot?

> *(***GERRY*** *will exit during:)*

SAUL. *(Who has just taken a sip, makes a terrible face.)* Not if you're lucky!

LOUISE. *(Offstage.)* I *heard* that, Saul Watson!

SAUL. *(Amiably.)* Then let it be a lesson to you!

(Offstage, we hear **LOUISE** *laugh.)*

POLLY. *(Sitting in center of sofa.)* I hope we get this act done tonight. Three days till dress rehearsal and we haven't even done a full run-through!

BILLY. Thank your friend *Phyllis* for *that*!

HENRY. You mustn't blame Phyllis, Billy – she's simply a perfectionist.

SMITTY. If she wasn't satisfied with the script, why did she submit it?

SAUL. Because if we'd picked some other show, she'd have had to wait till next *year* to get it done!

VIOLET. Why couldn't we do it as our *next* show?

BILLY. We've got our audiences pre-conditioned.

SAUL. "Brainwashed" is more like it!

POLLY. That's putting it rather strongly, Saul.

SAUL. It's the unvarnished truth. We never vary, season after season. We do a mystery, a comedy, a drama, and a musical, in that order, without fail.

VIOLET. Yes, but why?

HENRY. We started the theatre that way, and it just got to be a habit. For us *and* our patrons.

VIOLET. But what would be the harm if we mixed it up?

SAUL. It would confuse people. The comedy fans would come to the drama and laugh at all the tragic moments – and the musical fans would start beating time to the comedy – !

BILLY. Or sob during the mystery!

AGGIE. They may *still* do *that*!

GERRY. *(Re-enters with cup of coffee.)* Aggie! Whose side are you on, anyway?!

AGGIE. On the side of *sanity* – which doesn't do me much good around *here*!

(Exits toward coffee.)

SAUL. *(Drains his cup.)* Well, *I'm* all set. Anybody *else* ready to give it a go?

POLLY. Oh, relax, Saul. We're all *much* too tense, tonight. Why do we keep *snapping* at each other the way we do? This near the opening, we're usually kidding around and having a *marvelous* time!

BILLY. If you want *my* opinion, we're running scared.

SMITTY. Scared of what?

SAUL. In our own way, Smitty, we're just as perfection-oriented as our author. We want the show to be a smash, not a smash-up.

HENRY. Amen.

> *(**AGGIE** re-enters with empty tray, starts collecting cups.)*

POLLY. We'll get it. Somehow, no matter how awful a show may look in rehearsal, we always manage to bring it off.

GERRY. That's with a *printed* script, Polly. This typewritten stuff is okay, don't get me wrong – it's all the *revisions* that are killing us!

POLLY. But Phyllis gave her solemn word –

SAUL. It's the only kind of word she knows! I'll bet she's never giggled in her life!

VIOLET. And she promised the same thing *last* week, Polly, then showed up on Monday with three new scenes!

SAUL. I wish she wouldn't keep changing the identity of the murderer! I don't know whether to radiate menace or charm the pants off everyone!

GERRY. Well, you won't do *either* just *standing* there! Come on, everybody, positions!

> *(**AGGIE** will exit with the last of their cups during:)*

Let's see if we can't go through to the curtain without stopping.

> *(Will descend from stage and move toward her seat.)*

SMITTY. *(Starts offstage.)* We'd better! I've got to get home and study for a biology exam!

BILLY. Wait, Smitty! ...Gerry – are we taking it from the top, or where?

GERRY. Why don't we go back to Violet's line, when Smitty made her entrance too early, and do the page we left out?

> (**PLAYERS** *ad-lib assent, and get into their positions.*)

VIOLET. I can't remember what my line *is*!

SAUL. Aggie, throw her a cue!

AGGIE. *(Offstage.)* Just let me find the place...

> *(They wait a moment; then:)*

Okay, I found it. Violet, I'll feed you Billy's line, then you start.

VIOLET. Okay.

AGGIE. *(Offstage.)* "Ah, but Lady Margaret, he might have had motor trouble."

VIOLET. *(In character.)* "Yes, indeed. I do hope *he* hasn't had an – " wait, I'll get it.

POLLY. I certainly *hope* so!

GERRY. Quiet, Polly. Go on, Violet.

VIOLET. "...I do hope he hasn't had an *accident*! These roads can be treacherous at night."

SMITTY. *(Offstage.)* Is that where I – ?

GERRY. No, no! That was "treacherous"! Wait for "lecherous"!

SMITTY. *(Offstage.)* Oh, yeah. Sorry.

GERRY. *(After a silence.)* Well? Who *does* have the next line?

AGGIE. *(Offstage.)* It's Polly's.

POLLY. *(Straightens up.)* Oh, my! Let me see –

AGGIE. *(Offstage.)* It's –

POLLY. No, don't tell me! I'll get it!

VIOLET. *(Happy to return* **POLLY***'s earlier comment.)* I certainly *hope* so!

GERRY. Oh, for the love of – !

POLLY. I've got it, I've got it! Violet, would you – ?

VIOLET. *(Interrupts wearily with the cue line:)* "...roads can be treacherous at night!"

POLLY. "Don't say such a thing! It would make one think that perhaps there was some truth, after all, in that story about the curse!"

HENRY. "Nonsense, my dear. There's no such thing as a curse."

BILLY. "And yet – everyone who has ever owned the Delhi Diamond – " *(Stops.)* Gerry – does it *have* to be called that?! It sounds like it comes from a delicatessen!

POLLY. That's because you're not sounding the "h," Billy. "*Dell*-hee!" – not "Delly"!

SAUL. Polly, that "h" is silent! It *is* pronounced "Delly"!

SMITTY. *(Enters.)* Can't we *please* go on? I've got to study for that exam!

GERRY. No, wait, Smitty – Billy's got a point. It *does* sound like it belongs alongside the liverwurst – it looks all right when you read it in the script, but it sounds just plain silly!

SAUL. Okay, so call it the *"Calcutta* Diamond"!

POLLY. You can't *do* that! Phyllis Montague told me particularly that she chose that name for its lovely alliteration – "*Del*hi *Di*amond" –

SAUL. Okay, so we'll alliterate – we'll call it the "Calcutta Carbuncle"!

VIOLET. *Carbuncle?*

SAUL. Yeah. It's a big stone like a ruby – a garnet-cut whatchacallit – a cabochon!

VIOLET. Well, it *sounds* like a big *zit!*

SAUL. So do you!

GERRY. Saul! Stop it! There *must* be another gem we can use –

POLLY. You shouldn't tamper with Phyllis's dialogue – she won't like it.

GERRY. She'll like it a lot *less* if her "Delhi Diamond" gets a *laugh*!

HENRY. Gerry's right, dear. We *should* have a different name for it.

POLLY. *(Half convinced.)* Well –

BILLY. Hey, *I've* got it! Let's call it the "Ranchipur Ruby"!

SAUL. Hey, I *like* that! It's got class!

POLLY. But whatever will we tell Phyllis?!

SMITTY. Tell her she *rewrote* it that way! She's done so many revisions, she'll probably believe it!

> *(Exits.)*

GERRY. Well, let's hope so! Meanwhile – *children* – can we return to the play?!

BILLY. Okay, okay. Where was I – ?

AGGIE. *(Offstage.)* Hey, Gerry, should I write in that change, or not?

GERRY. You may as well – but do it in pencil, just in case.

AGGIE. *(Offstage.)* Gotcha. *(Beat.)* How do you spell "Ranchipur"?

GERRY. *(At wit's end.) Fake* it! Nobody has to *read* it but *you*! *(To* **BILLY***.)* Go ahead with your line – it's the one right after Lord Dudley scoffs at the curse.

BILLY. Oh, yeah... "And yet – everyone who has ever owned the Ranchipur Ruby has always met with a dreadful demise!"

POLLY. There! You see? I *knew* there was a reason for Phyllis's words. It's double-alliteration: "Delhi Diamond" and "dreadful demise"!

SAUL. Oh, who *gives* a damn?!

HENRY. See here, you can't talk to my wife like that!

GERRY. Henry, for once I agree with Saul! Who *gives* a damn! Billy, go on!

BILLY. Right! ... "And yet – everyone who has ever owned the Ranchipur Ruby has always met with a *rotten requiem!*"

(*All laugh except* **POLLY** *and* **HENRY**.)

SAUL. Aw, c'mon, Billy! You sound like an elocution teacher!

BILLY. (*Shrugs.*) So does Phyllis Montague!

POLLY. Now, really – !

VIOLET. It double-alliterates, doesn't it?

GERRY. Billy – don't. Leave the line's ending as written. Please?

BILLY. Oh, all right. " – has always met with a dreadful demise!"

VIOLET. (*Beat.*) Oh! *My* line! (*Into character.*) "But Percival doesn't own the diamond – " Oops, wait! " – the *ruby* anymore – not since he sold it to Lord Dudley for Lady Margaret's collection."

SAUL. "Nevertheless – Percival *did* own it – and that might be enough."

BILLY. "See here, Doctor Forbes – you are a man of science – surely *you* don't believe in curses?"

SAUL. "I only know there are strange things in the history of India – things which defy rational explanation."

HENRY. "Nonsense. Sheer poppycock. Superstitious drivel!"

SAUL. "Quite possibly, Lord Dudley – and yet – "

POLLY. "And yet – ?"

SAUL. "*Where* is Sir Percival?"

VIOLET. "Frankly, I'm *glad* he's not here!"

POLLY. "Why, Diana, what a thing to say!"

VIOLET. "I mean it. Sir Percival is – no gentleman."

HENRY. "Here, now, what are you saying?"

VIOLET. "When he looks at me – I feel as though his hands were moving all over my body."

POLLY. "But – he is a knight of the realm!"

VIOLET. "He is a disgusting toad. And such toads can be lecherous at night!"

> *(**SMITTY** enters.)*

SMITTY. "Begging your pardon, milord, but should we delay dinner any longer?"

> *(Phone rings.)*

GERRY. *(Comes to her feet.) Louise!* What are you *doing*?!

LOUISE. *(Offstage.)* Isn't that where the phone rings? ...Oh, wait! I turned two pages at once! Sorry about that!

POLLY. "Sorry," she says! If she does that during the performance – !

GERRY. She won't, Polly, she won't! Louise, you've got to be more careful!

LOUISE. *(Offstage.)* Look on the bright side. Now we know the phone bell works.

POLLY. That woman! I could – !

SAUL. No you couldn't. Louise has a black belt in karate.

POLLY. And how do you know *I* haven't?!

SAUL. They only go up to size forty-four!

GERRY. *(Apprehensively.)* Saul – ?

> *(But it is too late; **POLLY** comes to her feet so fast that the chair falls over backwards, and storms offstage with **HENRY** meekly in her wake, on:)*

POLLY. That does it! I'm through!

HENRY. Now, honey, you mustn't be hasty about this – !

> *(They are gone; remaining **PLAYERS** look accusingly at **SAUL**.)*

SAUL. *(Much abashed.)* I was only *kidding*...

LOUISE. *(Wanders onstage.)* What was that crash?

> *(Sees fallen chair.)*

Oh.

SAUL. I better go apologize...

(Hurries out after duo.)

VIOLET. *(Dispirited.)* What do we do now?

AGGIE. *(Comes onstage, script in hand.)* You can't work *around* her – she's got herself in damn near every scene.

BILLY. *(Righting chair and straightening "sofa.")* Not the love scene in Act Two. Maybe we could do that one.

VIOLET. Can't we wait till we have a real sofa? That metal's awfully hard to cuddle on.

GERRY. Aggie, when *do* we get the sofa?

AGGIE. We should've had it two days ago.

GERRY. Could you call and find out?

AGGIE. I could try.

(Exits.)

LOUISE. You want a look at that corridor wall, Gerry?

GERRY. *(Will get onto stage.)* Yes, I'd better. I'm worried about those braces.

LOUISE. You and me both. I've got six two-by-fours on it already, and the thing still flaps like a sail!

(They will move offstage during:)

SMITTY. Well, I guess I'll go hit the old biology book!

BILLY. You've got it *here*?

SMITTY. Why not? All the time I spend waiting to make my entrance, I could study for *three* exams!

(Exits.)

BILLY. Well, Violet, whattaya say – ?

VIOLET. Oh – all right.

(Gets up from "armchair," sits on "sofa.")

Ready when you are.

BILLY. *(Moves to point just inside right doorway.)* Okay. On your mark – get set – *(Into character.)* "Oh! Diana. I was seeking Lady Margaret."

VIOLET. "Lady Margaret is cutting roses in the garden, Stephen."

(Looks down demurely, folds her hands in her lap.)

"She – may not return for some time."

BILLY. "I see."

(Moves closer.)

"Would you mind if I waited for her...here?"

VIOLET. "Naturally not."

BILLY. "Might I...sit?"

VIOLET. "If you are so inclined."

BILLY. *(Sits beside her.)* "Diana – "

VIOLET. *(Eyes still downcast, turns head away.)* "Yes, Stephen – ?"

BILLY. "Would you take offense if I were to – to – ?"

VIOLET. "Stephen, what are you trying to say?"

BILLY. "Oh, dash it all, Diana, must we play at words?! You *know* the message that longs to cry out from within my heart!"

VIOLET. *(Raises her eyes, looks at him.)* "Is it possible – do I dare for a moment imagine – that the message in your heart is the selfsame message that cries out from within my own – ?"

BILLY. "Diana – do you mean – do I dare to dream – ?"

(Takes her hands.)

VIOLET. "Have a care, sir – have a care – you know that I am betrothed to another man!"

BILLY. "And yet – you do not draw away...?"

VIOLET. "Oh, Stephen – can you not reason out *why*?!"

BILLY. "I – I am almost afraid to!"

VIOLET. "Then *cease* your noble trepidations, Stephen Sellers. For – though I am a high-born lady – I am also a woman!"

BILLY. "Oh, Diana!"

(Kisses her lightly on the lips.)

VIOLET. "Oh, Stephen!"

(Lays her head against his shoulder.)

VIOLET. "If Doctor Forbes should come upon us – !"

BILLY. *"Hang* your illustrious fiancé! He shall not have you!"

(Kisses her again, a bit more firmly.)

"Oh, Diana – !"

VIOLET. Oh – Billy!

BILLY. Oh – Violet!

(And they go into a real clinch, clutching and caressing and swaying, the metal chairs rattling until:)

LOUISE. *(Enters.)* What's all that clattering – ?!

(They spring apart and come to their feet.)

Ha! No *wonder* you want a real sofa!

VIOLET. Now, Louise – !

LOUISE. I didn't see a thing. Not a thing.

(Gives a happy cackle of amusement and exits.)

VIOLET. Billy – do you think she suspects?!

BILLY. How could she? I didn't suspect, *myself,* till just a moment ago!

VIOLET. Oh, darling, neither did I!

(They almost embrace, but break decorously apart and try to look innocent as they hear:)

PHYLLIS. *(Offstage.) Yoo*-hoo – ?! Anybody *here* – ?!

VIOLET. Billy! That sounds like Miss Montague!

BILLY. Tonight? But she promised not to come back till dress rehearsal!

(Others reappear onstage via various routes, all wearing the same apprehensive look as our duo.)

GERRY. Did *you* all hear what *I* heard – ?

POLLY. It sounded like *Phyllis*!

SAUL. Probably with five new pages of dialogue for *you*!

POLLY. *(With patient forebearance.)* Saul – I just accepted *one* apology from you – do you want to have to make *another*?!

SAUL. *(Sincerely.)* Sorry, Polly.

> *(This time we can definitely pinpoint the source of the voice as emanating from the rear of the theatre:)*

PHYLLIS. *Yoo*-hoo! How *are* you all?!

> *(All turn and peer out into theatre, watching the progress of* **PHYLLIS MONTAGUE** *– a maiden lady of indeterminate age, probably anywhere between forty-two and fifty-seven – and especially noting the sheaf of papers she carries, as she hurries happily down the aisle toward the stage.)*

GERRY. Why – Phyllis – we weren't expecting you – at least, not tonight – !

PHYLLIS. Oh, I *know* I'm being a *naughty* girl, Geraldine, but I have so many new and good things to share with you all that I simply *couldn't* wait until the dress rehearsal!

SAUL. *(Wide-eyed, and absolutely frank.)* Well, *that's* a mercy!

> *(***PHYLLIS** *has gotten up onstage, now, and is moving along the row of people there, handing each an identical sheaf of stapled-together pages, during:)*

GERRY. Phyllis! *More* changes? We *open* in four nights!

PHYLLIS. That's why I decided not to wait until dress rehearsal to stop by. This would be much too much to have to learn in one night!

HENRY. What makes you think we can do it in *three*?

PHYLLIS. Oh, don't be a tease, Henry. It's really all very simple. I've simply added just *one* extra character and cut the love scene.

BILLY & VIOLET. *(In woeful unison.)* "*Cut* the *love* scene"?!

PHYLLIS. Perhaps I'm putting it too strongly – it's not precisely cut – just cut out of Act Two and moved back to Act One.

BILLY. Oh, well, that's not so bad.

PHYLLIS. Except it's no longer between Diana and Stephen.

VIOLET. Then – between who else?

AGGIE. Yeah, the Lord and Lady are already married –

SMITTY. You *can't* mean the Doctor and the *maid* – *can* you?

PHYLLIS. Oh, dear, perhaps I didn't make it clear. *Diana* still plays the scene – but now it's with Sir Percival!

GERRY. What? But Phyllis –

LOUISE. How can you do such a thing?

PHYLLIS. Oh, well, I got to thinking that perhaps a knight of the realm was a better catch for Diana than a mere rich commoner like Stephen, so –

LOUISE. Phyllis, I didn't say *why* – I said *how* can you do it? We don't *have* a Sir Percival in the play!

GERRY. Exactly! Everybody *refers* to him, all the time, but he never actually *appears*!

SAUL. Besides, it's kind of rough on *Diana* if you make that switch – considering that I *bump off* Percival before I show up at the house!

PHYLLIS. You *do*?

POLLY. Don't you even remember your own *plot*, Phyllis?

PHYLLIS. Yes, but I don't recall a *murder*...show me where it says so.

BILLY. We never actually *see* it done. But once we find that Percival has vanished, and then Rex has the famous gemstone Percival was bringing to the party, we figure out who *killed* him, see?

PHYLLIS. *(Pondering deeply.)* Murder. I never thought of it as a murder. I just thought that, well, Rex had picked Percival's pocket, and perhaps drained all the petrol from the tank of his car to keep him from the party. After all – murder is so – so –

GERRY. *Popular* with our *patrons*!

POLLY. And we're already *advertising* it as a murder mystery!

AGGIE. And we *do open* in *four nights,* Phyllis, for Pete's *sake*! It's a bit late to audition Percivals!

PHYLLIS. Oh, but I've written you all the loveliest new lines...!

>   *(Looks ready to weep.)*

Won't you – won't you at least have a *look* at them – ?

>   *(There is a pause, and an exchange of glances among the group, and then – since none of them is truly heartless – they all shrug and mumble some sort of assent, and start looking – just a bit warily – at the new pages.)*

VIOLET. *(Gasps.)* I'm *pregnant*!

>   *(Others react, of course.)*

BILLY. You're *what*?!

VIOLET. I mean *Diana* is!

>   *(Others evince great relief; she continues:)*

But who's the father?

PHYLLIS. That's on the third sheet.

>   *(All flip pages like mad; then:)*

AGGIE. Lord Dudley!

POLLY. *(Appalled.)* Henry!

HENRY. *(Patiently.)* Polly, don't be an idiot.

POLLY. Oh. Yes. But – it *was* a bit of a shock.

BILLY. This is crazy! Phyllis, how can Dudley be the father, when he and Diana have only just met?!

PHYLLIS. Oh, that's on the fifth sheet.

>   *(All flip pages again.)*

GERRY. *Amnesia?!*

PHYLLIS. Yes, because that explains why he doesn't remember their meeting.

SMITTY. But if she's carrying his child, *Diana* must remember something!

PHYLLIS. No, that's explained on page seven.

(Again all flip like crazy.)

You see, it was a very dark night, and –

GERRY. *(Closes up her sheaf, lets hand holding sheaf drop.)* Phyllis, this is totally *impossible*! The entire *thrust* of the plot is altered! Everybody has a brand new motivation for what they do!

PHYLLIS. Well, surely, with a little work –

LOUISE. In the next four *days*?!

SAUL. We couldn't do it in four *months*!

PHYLLIS. But – I've worked so hard – !

GERRY. And we *haven't*?! Phyllis, there's *no way* we can make these changes at this late date!

PHYLLIS. But they're such *little* changes!

BILLY. Little?! What about the ending? If Stephen is going to marry Diana, won't her pregnancy kind of put a *crimp* in the festivities?

PHYLLIS. Well, I'm working on that.

GERRY. *More* changes?! Phyllis Montague, do you have any notion how *hard* it is to do a play – even a play that *doesn't* change direction every three days?! This script should have been finalized three *weeks* ago!

POLLY. *(Who has been reading the new sheets.)* What's this?! Lady Margaret goes into *shock* at the news of Diana's pregnancy and loses the power of *speech*?!

SAUL. *(Brightens.)* Really? Say, maybe this version's not so bad *after* all!

GERRY. *(Warningly.)* Saul...!

SMITTY. And what about my *mother*?

GERRY. *(Distracted.)* What *about* your mother?

SMITTY. Well, when I first tried out for the part, my mother insisted on looking over the script because she didn't want me in a play full of sex! If Diana's pregnant, I'll have to quit the show.

PHYLLIS. But she's only *two months* pregnant – I mean, it's not going to *show* – ?!

SMITTY. Mother thinks ahead.

PHYLLIS. *(A little genteel blackmail.)* Well, of course, if you'd *all* rather not *do* my little play –

GERRY. *(Having none of it.)* Now, hold it *right* there, Phyllis! We all appreciate the chance to do a play for which we do not have to pay royalties – in fact, doing your show would put the theatre budget in the black for the first time in six months! However – when the play reading committee agreed to do this play of yours, it was on the basis of the *original* script! Now, *that* play we promised to do, and we will – but all this *new* stuff has nothing to *do* with that agreement – !

PHYLLIS. *(Trying to hide her dismay.)* You're telling me that you now feel free to *reject* my play – ?

GERRY. Not the play as *first* submitted, Phyllis – and I'll even allow you *all* the alterations you've *already* made – but this *last* batch is just too much!

PHYLLIS. *(One last stand.)* Do you have the authority to speak for the entire committee?

GERRY. No. But when I tell them it's either the *first* version or *no* version, I'll have their *unanimous* backing!

PHYLLIS. *(Trying to save face.)* Well, of course, if you really feel *strongly* about this matter, dear Geraldine –

> *(All simply stare at her; she wilts, and seeks an ally.)*

Polly! How do *you* feel about it – ?

POLLY. Well – I – it *is* rather close to opening night, Phyllis, and – and – of course, *perhaps* –

SAUL. *(Quietly.)* Remember – she cut *all* your speeches –

POLLY. *(Remembers.)* I'm with Gerry!

(Hands sheaf back to **PHYLLIS***; others all immediately do the same, until she holds an untidy stack, during:)*

VIOLET. Me, too!

BILLY. You bet!

SMITTY. Absolutely!

SAUL. Right on!

HENRY. I agree!

LOUISE. Thanks, anyway!

AGGIE. Nice try!

GERRY. Sorry, Phyllis!

PHYLLIS. *(Very annoyed and somewhat angry.)* All right. All right. Go ahead and *do* the original version. But if the show's *reviews* turn out to be a box office disaster – well – !

SAUL. We'll all remember who *wrote* the original.

PHYLLIS. Oh! *Oh!* OH!

(Slams her stack under one arm and storms off into the wings; all pause, listening, till we hear door slam.)

GERRY. Do you think – maybe – we were a little rough on her – ?

POLLY. She *did* take it rather hard...

HENRY. She said once at dinner that – she looks upon this play as her *child* –

POLLY. It's the only offspring she'll ever have –

HENRY. And when she tried to make that child a little prettier –

GERRY. Oh, dear! I wish you hadn't put it like that!

SAUL. Gerry, don't be a sap! Phyllis wasn't making her child *prettier* – she was giving it an extra *head*!

GERRY. *(Laughs, her good sense restored.)* You're right. Let's leave the kid alone and start learning to love it *as is*!

BILLY. *Now* you're talking!

AGGIE. Come on, everyone – you *came* here to rehearse – so let's *rehearse*!

LOUISE. *(Starts offstage.)* I'll give you all to the count of three – and if I don't hear some snappy dialogue, I'm picking up that *hammer* again!

AGGIE. *(Moving after **LOUISE**.)* And *I'll* hold the *nails*!

GERRY. *(Starts offstage as they exit.) I'm* grabbing another cup of coffee – *you* people pick up your long faces and get into character!

> *(Exits.)*

BILLY. *(Calls after her.)* Shall we take it from the top?

GERRY. *(Offstage.) Not* if you want to finish the act before *dawn*! Pick it up from Saul's line about the telegraph office.

SAUL. Right!

> *(Gets into character as **PLAYERS** get into places, and:)*

"Well – as a matter of fact – I don't have it. The message was phoned from the telegraph office."

BILLY. "Doris – have there been any telephone messages this evening?"

SAUL. "See here, you insolent young pup! Are you doubting my word?!"

POLLY. "Of course he isn't, Rex! Stephen, you should apologize to Doctor Forbes!"

BILLY. "Oh, I shall. As soon as Doris answers my question."

SMITTY. "No, sir."

POLLY. "What, are you quite sure?"

SMITTY. "The telephone has been out of order since this *afternoon,* mum."

BILLY. "Aha! And what do you say to *that,* Doctor Forbes?"

> *(The phone rings.)*

SAUL. "Does *that* answer your question?"

POLLY. "Stephen, I believe you owe Doctor Forbes an apology."

(Phone rings again.)

HENRY. "You had best answer that, Doris, before we owe the *caller* an apology, too!"

SMITTY. *(Moving to phone.)* "Yes, sir!"

(Answers.)

"Hello – ? ...Who? ...Why, yes, he is. Just a moment."

(Extends phone to HENRY.*)*

"It's for you, sir."

HENRY. *(As he takes phone.)* "Who is it, Doris?"

SMITTY. "Sir Percival."

SAUL. *(Aghast.)* "It *can't* be – ! ...I mean – "

BILLY. *(Calmly.)* "Yes, Doctor? Exactly what *do* you mean?"

SAUL. "Why – I – I – "

*(*GERRY, *sipping coffee, appears in upstage doorway, watching group, and* AGGIE *appears similarly outside upstage window, during:)*

HENRY. *(On phone.)* "Hello? ...What? ...Ah! Yes, I see... Yes, thank you! Thank you very much!"

(Hangs up.)

POLLY. "Why – Dudley – you look so strange! What did Percival *say*?"

*(*HENRY *opens his mouth to reply, but before he can:)*

GERRY. Excuse me, just a moment –

*(*PLAYERS *pause and all look toward her.)*

VIOLET. Did we do something wrong?

GERRY. No, of course not. But I wanted to see what you were all *doing* when the phone rang. Could we take it back a few lines – ?

AGGIE. It's a long way to the end of the act, Gerry. Do you think – ?

GERRY. This will only take a moment, Aggie. Just back up to Smitty's line about the phone, okay – ?

(**PLAYERS** *ad-lib assent, shift into positions, and:*)

SMITTY. "The telephone has been out of order since this *afternoon*, mum."

BILLY. "Aha! And what do you say to *that*, Doctor Forbes?"

(*And from the phone comes the sound of a musical auto-horn [C-E-low G-E]; All react.*)

ALL. *Louise!*

LOUISE. (*Offstage.*) Sorry! I forgot to wind the tape back! Hang on – *now* I've got it!

(**PLAYERS** *get into position, and:*)

BILLY. "Aha! And what do you say to *that*, Doctor Forbes?'

(*And from the phone comes the sound of a gun shot.*)

LOUISE. (*Offstage.*) Oops! Wrong place!

AGGIE. (*Shakes her head.*) And only four more days till opening night!

(**PLAYERS** *all sag, and we hear:*)

LOUISE. (*Offstage.*) *I'll* get it!

(*Sound of auto-horn.*)

Oops!

(*Sound of gunshot.*)

Sorry!

(*Sound of screech of tires.*)

Damn it all to hell!

(*And as we hear – in quick succession – the sounds of, in order, auto-horn, thundering footsteps, screech of tires, gunshot-scream-gunshot-scream-gunshot-scream – during which the dispirited group all sag lower and lower and lower – .*)

(*The curtain falls.*)

ACT II

(The set as we last saw it, except that the upstage corridor wall is now in place, and there is a real sofa and a real armchair in place of the folding chairs in Act One.)

(Note: If you desire a more radical transformation, you might also have lacked, in Act One, the window drapes, the tray of liquor bottles and glasses on the sideboard, and the books – or some of them – on the bookshelves; these items will be in place, now, of course, in this act.)

(Just before curtain rise, have the house lights dim halfway and the curtain closed until counterindicated. When lights have dimmed, we hear from the rear of house:)

GERRY. Louise? Why isn't the curtain open?

*(**GERRY** will come down aisle to her place, during:)*

LOUISE. *(Offstage.)* There's a draft up here. The curtain keeps some of it out!

GERRY. That's because someone left the front door open. I closed it.

(Curtain starts to open.)

LOUISE. *(Offstage.)* Why are theatres always drafty backstage?!

AGGIE. *(Offstage.)* They're designed that way on purpose. The breeze comes in handy if the play smells!

*(**GERRY** sits in front row as curtain comes fully open.)*

GERRY. I don't suppose you have a *particular* play in mind, Aggie – ?

AGGIE. *(Off. Laughs.)* Don't say I didn't warn you!

> (**GERRY** *laughs, and then* **BILLY** *steps onstage in costume.*)

> (Note: Costumes for the play-within-the-play are a bit old-fashioned – Edwardian clothing for the men, evening gowns for **VIOLET** and **POLLY**, and a black dress with short white apron and cap for **SMITTY**.)

BILLY. Gerry, do we have to wear makeup tonight?

GERRY. Well, I don't care so much about the men – but I did want to see how the women look – especially their hairdos.

BILLY. *(Starting off.)* I think they're using wigs.

GERRY. I've *seen* the wigs – I want to see how they look *wearing* them.

BILLY. I'll tell 'em.

> (As he exits, he passes **AGGIE** just coming onstage.)

AGGIE. *(Flips a thumb upstage.)* How do you like the wall?

GERRY. Well – it looks okay on *this* side – but how much space is there to move behind it?

AGGIE. If everyone's careful, they'll have about two inches clearance on either side –

> (Lowers her voice, leans forward to add confidentially:)

Except for *Polly*, of course!

GERRY. How's she going to get from the garden to the prop table for the roses she brings onstage?

AGGIE. She doesn't have to. I'm going to keep the roses on *that* side of the stage. I told her it was to simplify things for her – but I didn't tell her what I simplifying.

GERRY. That's good thinking. We've got to keep her in a happy mood. She nearly walked out *again,* last night, thanks to Saul Watson!

AGGIE. *(Chuckles at the memory.)* You gotta admit – he was pretty funny!

GERRY. Yes, but his sense of humor cost us a half hour! At least, I got him to *swear* he'll say that Lord Dudley is off to *"have a word* with Lady Margaret" – not *"chew the fat"* with her!

AGGIE. Yeah, but even if he behaves himself in rehearsal, how do we know what he's gonna do when the show's in performance?

GERRY. I don't want to think about it. I'm already having nightmares!

AGGIE. I'm surprised you can sleep at all. Tomorrow night, the whole thing will be out of your hands. All you can do *then* is stand in the wings and *pray*...there's not enough *room* to *kneel!*

GERRY. Maybe I'll just spend opening night in some cozy bar. In another town.

> (**LOUISE** *enters, carrying a sparkling necklace.)*

LOUISE. Hey, how do you like *this* thing, Gerry? Looks *real,* doesn't it?!

GERRY. It certainly does. It was nice of Phyllis to lend it to us for the show. Costume jewelry that good is awfully expensive.

AGGIE. Have you figured out yet what to do about the central stone? We still haven't told Phyllis we've nixed her "Delhi Diamond" – how are we going to pass this thing off as a ruby?

GERRY. As a matter of fact, *Billy* came up with the solution to that: From now on, it's known as the "White Ruby of Ranchipur"!

LOUISE. *(Moving with necklace toward wall safe.) Is* there such a thing as a white ruby?

GERRY. (*Wearily.*) There is, *now!*

> (**LOUISE** *and* **AGGIE** *laugh;* **LOUISE** *opens door of safe.*)

And *please* keep that in a safe place between performances, Louise. We wouldn't want it to get misplaced, or stolen!

LOUISE. Don't worry. I figure this necklace is our ace in the hole – Phyllis will preoccupy herself worrying about *it* instead of the *play!*

AGGIE. There's something to *that,* all right.

GERRY. (*As* **LOUISE** *places necklace inside safe.*) You know, I'd feel a lot easier if that safe had a back to it. A person could tiptoe up in back of the flat and pick the necklace right up.

LOUISE. I could nail one on – but I'd have to take the safe down, first – and that would mean repainting the flat.

GERRY. Why would you have to take it down?

LOUISE. Because if I hammer on the back, and the front is where it is now, the whole thing'll tear loose from the flat and fall on the stage.

AGGIE. Tell you what – I'm not doing much except prompting, once this curtain's up. Why don't I just hang onto the thing, and then *hand* it to Saul when he reaches into the safe?

GERRY. Would you *mind,* Aggie? It'd set my mind at rest.

AGGIE. No trouble at all.

LOUISE. (*Will retrieve necklace and re-close safe, on:*) Well, you'd better practice it, then – tonight's your only chance before the opening.

AGGIE. (*Takes necklace.*) Easy as pie. But the practice can't hurt.

LOUISE. (*To* **GERRY.**) You ready for the mob, yet?

GERRY. I guess so – if they're all in costume.

LOUISE. Well, if they're not, it's their tough luck. (*Calls.*) Hey! Everybody onstage!

(We hear ad-libs akin to "Okay!", "Coming!" and such, from the PLAYERS, and then they come on, all in costume – except that VIOLET is carrying her costume wig.)

GERRY. Line up along the front of the stage, will you? I want to see how you all look. The costumes *seem* to fit all right...

(They line up while she's speaking.)

(Note: This will also be the curtain call lineup, and goes thusly, starting at stage left: SAUL, VIOLET, HENRY, POLLY, BILLY, SMITTY.)

POLLY. I think mine's just a little bit too small for me...

(Then, as if expecting the worst after this lovely straight line, PLAYERS all turn their heads to look at SAUL.)

SAUL. *(Since their stares are as good as any commentary from him.)* I *didn't* say a *word*!

POLLY. And you'd better not!

GERRY. *(Annoyed.)* Polly, be fair! It's one thing if he *picks* on you – but if you're going to blow up every time you think he *might* say something – !

POLLY. *(Abashed.)* Yes. You're right. I'm sorry, Saul. Just – rehearsal jitters, I guess.

SAUL. No problem.

GERRY. Good. Now – turn around, all of you, slowly, so I can see what you look like in back...

(They do so, stopping once they're faced upstage.)

Mmm – yes – yes – yes, you all look fine...oh, wait a minute! Violet, why aren't *you* wearing a bustle like Polly?

POLLY. *(Turns to face GERRY.)* I'm not *wearing* a bustle!

GERRY. Oh! Oh, dear, I'm sorry!

POLLY. *(Unexpectedly, laughs.)* *You're* sorry!

(Others all laugh, then, and an atmosphere of good humor floods the stage; remaining **PLAYERS** *now face front again.)*

GERRY. Violet – why aren't you wearing that wig?

VIOLET. It's too big. Let me show you –

(Slips it on, and we see that it sits low on her brow, so that we can barely see her eyes.)

See? I look like a British sheepdog!

GERRY. Can't you pad it, or take a tuck in it, or something?

VIOLET. I'll think of something. I didn't have time, just now.

GERRY. Okay. Well, you're going to all *look* just *fine!* ...Now suppose we see how well you can *act!*

AGGIE. Positions for Act One – ?

GERRY. I guess we may as well start, yes.

*(**PLAYERS** start getting into position.)*

LOUISE. *(Starting off.)* You want to do it with the curtain?

GERRY. Yes, I do. I want *everything* just as if this were the *performance!*

PHYLLIS. *(Offstage.) Yoo*-hoo – !

(All react.)

AGGIE. Gerry, I think you just got your wish.

LOUISE. In spades!

*(**LOUISE** and **AGGIE** exit as **PHYLLIS** enters, opposite.)*

PHYLLIS. Oh, Geraldine, I have the most dreadful news. We're going to have to change the name of my play!

GERRY. What? We can't, Phyllis! The programs are all printed, and the publicity's been mailed out –

PHYLLIS. But we must! I've just discovered that there is a *movie* with the *same* title – *Murder Most Foul!*

POLLY. Phyllis, no one in the audience is likely to be confused. They can *see* this isn't a *movie!*

SAUL. Right! In a movie, no one forgets their lines.

(**PLAYERS** *give him a woebegone look.*)

SMITTY. Don't *say* things like that, Saul! I'm having enough trouble already!

PHYLLIS. Oh, I *do* hope you are *joking,* Marla!

BILLY. *Who?* ...Oh! I almost forgot your *real* name, Smitty.

SMITTY. No one ever uses it – except my mother.

SAUL. And Phyllis.

PHYLLIS. Oh, but I think nicknames are so vulgar, Saul. Don't you?

SAUL. I'm the wrong guy to ask, Phyl.

GERRY. (*Quickly, before* **PHYLLIS** *can quite become angry.*) *Phyllis* – I'm *so* glad you're here tonight, because – you can be a great *help* to us all.

> (**PHYLLIS**, *very pleased, steps forward, so that she cannot see the dismay on the faces of the* **PLAYERS**, *during:*)

PHYLLIS. Really? How?

GERRY. (*Realizing she's trapped herself, invents:*) Uh – why – you can listen to the lines, and see that everyone is doing them properly!

AGGIE. (*Steps onstage, script in hand.*) And where does that leave *me*?

GERRY. Oh, Aggie, I didn't mean the *words,* exactly – I meant all the – uh – subtle little *nuances* of their *interpretation*!

AGGIE. (*Waves script mildly.*) The ones you forgot to tell *me* to mark down – ?

GERRY. (*Wearily.*) Yes.

PHYLLIS. Shall I sit out there beside *you* – ?

GERRY. *No!* ...That is – uh – I make *notes* all the time during rehearsal. I might distract you.

AGGIE. (*Starts off.*) Louise, have you got a *chair* for our *playwright* back there – ?

> (*Exits while we hear:*)

LOUISE. (*Offstage.*) If *you've* got a *dustrag*!

PHYLLIS. *(Moving off after* **AGGIE**.*)* Oh, this is thrilling! Simply thrilling!

    (Exits, and we hear immediately:)

SAUL. *(To* **GERRY**, *in a lowered voice.)* You got any *other* nice little surprises for us? *I* could use a thrill right now.

GERRY. *(Same level.)* It'll be okay, Saul. Don't lose your temper.

BILLY. *(Same level.)* What the hell are "nuances"?!

SAUL. *(Same level.)* Don't ask. Just grit your teeth and pray you've *got* 'em!

POLLY. *(To* **GERRY**, *same level.)* I thought you wanted us to go straight through without interruption?! With *Phyllis* back there listening for *nuances* – !

SAUL. *(Same level.)* Cheer up. Maybe Louise will drop a sandbag on her.

PHYLLIS. *(Off. Trills blithely.)* I'm read-y...!

GERRY. *(Sits back and sinks down apprehensively.)* Okay! Louise – close the damn – close the curtain, and we'll start!

    (Curtain starts to close as **PLAYERS** *move into position.)*

LOUISE. *(Offstage.)* You want the *music,* too?

GERRY. Of course! Everything exactly like the performance!

    (Curtain completes its close during:)

AGGIE. *(Offstage.)* Everybody hold your places during the music – !

SMITTY. I'm *offstage* when the curtain rises. I don't *have* a place.

SAUL. *(Now masked from our view by the closed curtain.)* You're *lucky*!

AGGIE. *(Offstage.)* Quiet, everybody!

    (Music – something dark and mysterious – starts.)

GERRY. The house lights! Louise, dim the house lights!

(Lights in theatre dim, fully, and will remain down for remainder of this act.)

That's fine, Louise! Do it like that at the opening – right after the music starts!

LOUISE. *(Offstage.)* Gotcha!

(Music finishes on a loud, ominous chord; curtain opens.)

(Note: The Act One of Murder Most Foul *tableau is:* **HENRY** *at the sideboard pouring a drink,* **VIOLET** *at the bookcase between upstage window and doorway, her back to us, seeking a book, and* **SMITTY** *using a featherduster on the front of the wall safe.)*

SMITTY. *(As she dusts.)* "Lord Dudley, will there be anyone at dinner tonight besides Sir Percival the famous archaeologist, Doctor Rex Forbes the famous scientist, and Stephen Sellers the famous millionaire?"

HENRY. "Other than myself and Lady Margaret, my wife, and the lovely socialite Diana Lassiter, here...no, Doris."

SMITTY. *(Starts toward stage right doorway, since she was only onstage to ladle out vital information to the audience.)* "That's what I *thought*."

(Exits.)

HENRY. *(Has his drink, holds it as he turns toward* **VIOLET**.*)* "I say, Diana, have you yet located that book on famous jewels of India that I told you must be there on the shelf?"

VIOLET. *(Who has been running a forefinger back and forth on the selfsame shelf during the opening lines, abruptly stops at a certain book.)* "Ah, yes! Here it is!"

(Takes book, turns downstage, flips it open at its very center, and immediately reacts to what she sees there.)

"Oh! I say, Lord Dudley – you didn't tell me there was a *curse* on the famous White Ruby of Ranchipur – ?!"

PHYLLIS. *(Offstage.)* The *what*?!

GERRY. It's *all* right, Phyllis, it's all *right*!

PHYLLIS. *(Steps onstage.)* But that's supposed to be the Delhi Diamond!

GERRY. We had to change it, Phyllis.

PHYLLIS. For what *possible* reason?!

SAUL. *(Offstage.)* It looked silly next to the liverwurst!

PHYLLIS. *(Looks uncertainly toward direction of his voice.)* *What* liverwurst? There's no *liverwurst* in *my* play!

VIOLET. We just wanted to *keep* it that way.

PHYLLIS. I beg your pardon?

GERRY. Phyllis! Trust me! Please go back off the stage, and Aggie will explain the change to you.

PHYLLIS. But – ?

GERRY. *Please*, Phyllis? We *open* tomorrow night!

PHYLLIS. Well – I – oh, very well, very well!

(Exits; **GERRY** *sinks back into seat.)*

GERRY. Go ahead with the show, people.

SMITTY. *(Offstage.)* From the top? I already put the featherduster away.

GERRY. No, no, no! Right from where we broke.

HENRY. Oh, all right. Violet – would you – ?

VIOLET. Oh, sure. *(Into character.)* "...the famous White Ruby of Ranchipur – ?!"

HENRY. "Fiddlesticks! A lot of hogwash! Damned superstitious rot!"

VIOLET. *(Will close book and put it back on shelf as she speaks.)* "But the book distinctly says that Lord Clyde Fortescue, the first owner of the Del – the White Ruby of Ranchipur – " *(Stops.)* Gerry, can I just say "ruby"?! I hate to say the whole mouthful every time!

GERRY. Yes, yes, yes! Just go *on*, go *on*!

VIOLET. *(Back into character.)* " – distinctly says that Lord Clyde Fortescue, the first owner of the ruby, was found floating in his tub, in his own blood! And the next owner, Sir Giles Renfrew, had no sooner purchased the ruby from Lord Clyde's estate, when *he* was found in his stables, trampled to death by his favorite horse! And the *next* owner – "

HENRY. "Balderdash! Nonsense! A lot of old wives' tales!"

VIOLET. "How *can* it be? They *are* all dead – aren't they?"

HENRY. "Yes, but consider: I bought the ruby this morning – and I'm fine!"

> (**HENRY** *suddenly puts a hand to his head and sways.*)

VIOLET. "Lord Dudley – is anything wrong?"

HENRY. "No-no. Nothing. Just one of my beastly attacks."

VIOLET. "How long have you had them?"

HENRY. "Since this morning."

VIOLET. "You don't suppose – ?"

HENRY. "Ridiculous! Sheer coincidence! Merest chance!"

SMITTY. *(Steps into room.)* "Doctor Forbes is here, Lord Dudley."

HENRY. "Ah! It is your fiancé, Diana!" *(To* GERRY.*)* That's a pretty dumb line, isn't it? She *knows* he's her fiancé.

PHYLLIS. *(Offstage.)* But the audience doesn't!

SAUL. Why don't I just wear a signboard?

PHYLLIS. *(Offstage.)* Now, really, Saul!

GERRY. Will you all stop your gabbing and get on with the *play*?! It's far too late to make alterations now!

HENRY. Oh, all right. "...It is your fiancé, Diana!"

VIOLET. "Yes, being engaged to the world-famous scientist has made me the envy of all the girls in England!"

HENRY. "Ah, but a lovely belle like you deserves to have a ring!"

VIOLET. Speaking of dumb lines – !

GERRY. Violet – !

PHYLLIS. *(Offstage.)* That line is *supposed* to be light-hearted. The merriment provides emotional contrast with the atmosphere of terror.

SMITTY. That's the general *atmosphere,* all right.

GERRY. Will you all *please* – ?!

VIOLET. Yes, yes, yes! *(Into character.)* "You flatter me, Lord Dudley."

HENRY. "Doris, will you show the gentleman in?"

SMITTY. "At once, milord!"

>   *(She exits and* **SAUL** *enters.)*

SAUL. *(Bows, briefly.)* "Lord Dudley. Diana."

HENRY. "I'm sure you young people will want to be alone."

>   *(Starts toward upstage doorway.)*

"I'll just toddle off to my room and putter about."

GERRY. Not that exit, Henry! That goes to the kitchen and the maid's quarters!

HENRY. Oh, that's right.

>   *(Starts toward right doorway, but pauses short of exit.)*

Of course, she's quite a good looking maid – !

POLLY. *(Offstage.)* Henry!

HENRY. Only joking, dear.

SMITTY. *(Offstage.)* You mean I'm *not* good looking?

HENRY. Uh – well – um –

GERRY. Henry, just *finish* your line and *go!*

HENRY. Saul's got a line, first.

SAUL. I have? Oh! Right! ... "Really, Lord Dudley, you needn't go."

HENRY. "Nonsense. I was once in love, myself!"

POLLY. *(Offstage.)* Why does he say that in the past tense?!

GERRY. Polly, please – !

POLLY. *(Offstage.)* Sorry.

>   *(**HENRY** exits; **SAUL** moves to **VIOLET** and embraces her.)*

SAUL. "My dearest darling!"

VIOLET. "My sweet!"

(They kiss, lightly, then stand apart.)

SAUL. "My darling, I have a little surprise – "

(Reaches into his pocket, then slumps.)

Oh, damn!

GERRY. What's the matter?

SAUL. Forgot the stupid necklace!

(Starts offstage.)

Aggie – ?!

AGGIE. *(Steps on, extending necklace.)* Here. Sorry about that.

GERRY. Aggie, as stage manager, you're supposed to make certain everyone has all their props!

AGGIE. I know, I know. Phyllis was talking to me about "nuances" and I missed Saul's entrance.

GERRY. Phyllis – you really mustn't chat backstage when people have work to do.

PHYLLIS. *(Offstage.)* I do apologize, Geraldine. I forgot Agnes had things to do.

AGGIE. My fault for not reminding her.

(Exits, on:)

"Agnes"! Ye gods!

SAUL. Pick it up from where we left off?

GERRY. Good a spot as any.

SAUL. "My darling, I have a little surprise – the White Ruby of Ranchipur!"

VIOLET. "Oh! How incredibly lovely it is! Might I – try it on?"

SAUL. "Not afraid of the curse?"

VIOLET. "Well – not *very* much... May I – please – ?"

SAUL. "Certainly you shall. Here, allow me..."

(She turns, he hangs it about her neck, then turns her around to face him.)

"It *is* lovely – in such a lovely *setting*!"

VIOLET. (*Lowers her eyes demurely, turns partly away.*) "Oh, Rex, what a thing to say – !"

SAUL. "I cannot decide which is lovelier, you or that fabulous gem."

VIOLET. "I simply must see myself in it – let me go find a mirror!"

> (*Starts toward right doorway, but stops as* **POLLY** *enters.*)

POLLY. "Diana! That necklace! How dare you! Take it off at once!"

VIOLET. "Lady Margaret! I was only – "

POLLY. "Take it off, I say! This instant!"

SAUL. (*Helps* **VIOLET** *undo clasp.*) "Here, now, Lady Margaret, there's surely no harm done...?"

POLLY. "No harm, you say? How could you endanger the life of this dear girl – and your own fiancée!"

VIOLET. "Oh, I don't believe in that silly curse, Lady Margaret! After all, this *is* the twentieth century!"

> (**VIOLET** *suddenly places the back of one hand to her forehead and sways.*)

SAUL. "Diana! Are you all right?"

VIOLET. "Yes – yes, I think so. It was just momentary – the room seemed to dip – my head started to spin – oh, but I'm quite all right, now."

POLLY. (*Takes necklace from* **SAUL.**) "I shall place this where it can do no more harm!"

> (*Moves toward wall safe.*)

SAUL. "Aren't you being silly, Lady Margaret?"

POLLY. (*Twirling dial of safe to open it.*) "Perhaps I am. But it is better to be safe than sorry!"

SAUL. "Should you not at least wait until Lord Dudley has seen his newest possession?"

POLLY. "He shall see it in good time – when I feel brave enough to wear it. And do not forget – he purchased it for me – so it is in actuality mine to deal with as I choose!"

(Has safe open, thrusts necklace within – and we hear necklace clatter to floor beyond open back of safe.)

Oh, dear, I pushed it too far!

PHYLLIS. *(Pops onstage.)* Do you mean to say there's no *back* on that thing?!

AGGIE. *(Enters, crosses to french doors, where she will exit during her line.)* My fault, my fault! I forgot I was supposed to be back there to grab the damned thing!

GERRY. Aggie, I hope you're making *notes* of all these things!

AGGIE. *(Offstage.)* Sure, sure. I just keep forgetting to *read* them!

POLLY. *(Wandering disconsolately away from safe.)* We'll *never* be ready by tomorrow night! Never! We're here almost an hour already, and we're not even halfway through the first act!

AGGIE. *(Enters carrying necklace.)* And we've only had two rehearsals of the third! And that's the most important act in the show!

BILLY. *(Steps onstage.)* Aggie's right. That's the act we're all really panicky about!

VIOLET. Why don't we *do* that act, right now! It's hard to do everything that comes before it, with that act hanging over our heads – if we felt more confident about it, I'm sure –

GERRY. All right, all right! *Anything* to get this show nailed down! Let's *do* the third act, get our confidence, and then run all three acts as fast as we can.

SMITTY. *(Steps onstage.)* How long will that take? My mother doesn't like me out too late on a school night. I just barely passed that biology exam.

GERRY. The sooner we begin, the sooner we'll finish! Come on, let's get moving!

*(All ad-lib assent; **PLAYERS** get into Act Three places, and **NON-PLAYERS** leave the stage.)*

LOUISE. *(Offstage.)* Do you want it with the curtain?

GERRY. Not now, Louise! Wait'll we're running the entire show.

LOUISE. *(Offstage.)* Okay, but hang on a second while I find the right spot on my tape!

GERRY. You've got nothing till that phone bell. Find your place while we run the act!

LOUISE. *(Offstage.)* Well, I'll do my best!

GERRY. Go ahead, everybody. Top of Act Three!

*(**PLAYERS** brace themselves; then:)*

PHYLLIS. *(Off. A cry of triumph.)* I've *got* it!

*(**PLAYERS** all lurch like standees on a streetcar which has come to an abrupt stop; **PHYLLIS** rushes onstage.)*

GERRY. Phyllis, you *can't* just interrupt *rehearsal* this way – !

PHYLLIS. But I've solved the problem of the liverwurst!

SAUL. Damn it, that's *already* been solved!

PHYLLIS. There's no need to use *profanity*, Saul!

SAUL. That's what *you* think!

PHYLLIS. *Please* hear me out – I was *so* concerned with the loss of my lovely double-alliteration...!

GERRY. *(Anything to get the show rolling.)* All right, all right! Let's hear the solution, but be quick!

PHYLLIS. *(Excitedly.)* We don't have to say "Delhi Diamond" – we call it the "Darjeeling Diamond"! Do you see? It's still named after a town in India, but now –

GERRY. I get it, I get it, thank you very much, we'll make the change, now please get off the stage and I don't want to see or hear you again until we've finished rehearsing this act, okay?!

PHYLLIS. You don't have to get huffy about it!

(Nose in air, exits from stage.)

GERRY. Has everybody got the new name for that stupid gem?

> (**PLAYERS** *al-lib assent.*)

Fine! Now – take it from the top of Act Three – and no stopping!

LOUISE. *(Offstage.)* What do you want to bet?

GERRY. *Please*, Louise – !

LOUISE. *(Offstage.)* Okay. Just thought it was a great opportunity to pick up some extra cash!

GERRY. *(Just short of a roar.)* Places! Everybody! And the *next* person who interrupts *dies*! I don't mean get-yelled-at... I don't mean chewed-out... I mean *dies*!

> (*Terrified* **PLAYERS** *brace themselves in position.*)

AGGIE. *(Offstage.)* On your marks – get set – *go*!

> (*Out of sheer panic,* **PLAYERS** *will say all the following play-within-the-play lines at frantic double-speed, with heightened emotion in their tones, and physical movements correspondingly extra-quick, akin to players in a sped-up movie film.*)

VIOLET. "Ah, Lord Dudley, you give the most charming parties in the whole of England!"

HENRY. "You are too kind, Diana. A pity Sir Percival could not be here."

POLLY. "Do you know – I'm *worried* about Percival! He's never accepted an invitation to one of our parties and then not shown up – at least, not without sending word."

BILLY. "Ah, but Lady Margaret, he might have had motor trouble."

VIOLET. Yes, indeed. I do hope he hasn't had an *accident*! These roads can be treacherous at night."

> (**SMITTY** *rushes on, realizes she's early, gives a little gasp, then rushes out again;* **POLLY** *becomes distracted.*)

POLLY. Uh – I – oh, damn it all to hell!

> *(Starts to cry, covers her face.)*

GERRY. *(Stands up.)* Wait. Please. This is all my fault. I should be providing you with a pleasant atmosphere to work in, not strike terror into all your hearts. Just – take it from where you're at – and slow it down a little, okay – ?

SAUL. Does that mean you're not going to kill Polly?

GERRY. *(With a slight edge.)* Yes. But don't *you* start feeling too secure!

SAUL. *(Takes a slight backstep.)* Uh – right.

GERRY. *(Resumes her seat.)* Go ahead, Polly. The roads can be treacherous at night...

POLLY. *(A bit recovered.)* My – my mind's gone blank. I can't think. I –

AGGIE. *(Off. Feeding the line in soothing tones.)* Don't-say-such-a-thing-it-would-make-one-think –

POLLY. Oh, yes, of course! *(Back into character, at normal speed.)* "Don't say such a thing! It would make one think that perhaps there was some truth, after all, in that story about the curse!"

HENRY. "Nonsense, my dear. There's no such thing as a curse."

BILLY. "And yet – everyone who has ever owned the Delhi – the ruby – the –" Wait, I'll get it – ! "...the *Darjeeling* Diamond – has always met with a dreadful demise!"

PHYLLIS. *(Offstage.)* Beautiful! Just beautiful!

EVERYBODY ELSE. *PHYLLIS!*

PHYLLIS. *(Offstage.)* Sorry.

VIOLET. "But Percival doesn't own the diamond – the ruby – the *diamond* – anymore – not since he sold it to Lord Dudley for Lady Margaret's correction – connection – confection – ?!"

AGGIE. *(Offstage.)* Collection!

VIOLET. " – collection."

SAUL. "Nevertheless – Percival *did* own it – and that might be enough."

BILLY. "See here, Doctor Fubbs – *Forbes* – !"

GERRY. Stop! ...Everybody take a deep breath and relax.

> (**PLAYERS** *all do so.*)

Fine. Now just go on, and enjoy yourselves!

BILLY. " – you are a man of science – surely *you* don't believe in curses?"

SAUL. "I only know there are strange things in the history of India – things which defy rational explanation."

HENRY. "Nonsense. Sheer pockycop – *pock*-ee-cop – !" *Aaaaagh!* "Poppycock! ...Superstitious drivel!"

SAUL. "Quite poppably –" Oh, damn it, *damn it*, DAMN IT!

GERRY. *(Amiably.)* Relax. You're all still too tense. Slow and easy does it.

SAUL. *(Takes a breath, continues.)* "Quite *possibly*, Lord Dudley – and yet – "

POLLY. "And yet – ?"

SAUL. *"Where* is Sir Percival?"

VIOLET. "Frankly, I'm *glad* he's not here!"

POLLY. "Why, Diana, what a thing to say!"

VIOLET. "I mean it. Sir Percival is – no gentleman."

HENRY. "Here, now, what are you saying?"

VIOLET. *(Without noticing that she's blowing her line.)* "When he looks at me – I feel as though his pants were moving all over my body."

> (Other **PLAYERS** *guffaw almost convulsively, turning away from her, unable to control their laughter.*)

What's the matter?

GERRY. It's his "hands," Violet, his "hands"!

VIOLET. Isn't that what I said?

BILLY. *(A bit more in control.)* You said "pants."

VIOLET. Oh!

(Starts to giggle.)

GERRY. Look, everyone, fun is fun, but we *would* like Smitty to get home sometime before *dawn!*

VIOLET. Right. I'm sorry.

> *(Her face will twitch a bit, as will those of the other* **PLAYERS**, *as she says her line correctly – but we all know what they are remembering.)*

"...I feel as though his *hands* were moving all over my body."

POLLY. *(Still in the throes of that blown version.)* "B-but – he is a knight of the – "

> *(Suppressing a laugh, makes a sound like a raspberry; other* **PLAYERS** *break up helplessly.)*

GERRY. *(Sternly, quietly.)* That's it – laugh it up – we'll see just how funny you think this is tomorrow night...!

> *(This sobers them; they regain control, fast.)*

POLLY. "...a knight of the realm!"

VIOLET. "He is a disgusting toad. And such toads can be lecherous at night!"

> *(There is a pause;* **PLAYERS** *slowly, covertly, look toward still-empty right doorway; then* **SMITTY** *gallops onstage, only about two seconds late.)*

SMITTY. "Begging-your-pardon-milord – "

GERRY. Take it easy, take it easy, you'll be just fine.

SMITTY. *(A bit slower.)* " – but should we delay dinner any longer?"

HENRY. "Mmm – no, I think not. Can't wait for Percival forever."

> *(Moves toward* **POLLY**.)

"Shall we, my dear?"

POLLY. "I suppose so. But – don't you think someone should call Percival's flat and ascertain the reason for his absence?"

BILLY. *(Moves around armchair to take* **VIOLET**'s *arm as she rises.)* "Do you know – that might be a sound idea. There is something distinctly odd about all of this."

VIOLET. "All of what, Stephen?"

BILLY. "This business about Percival and the necklace. He *did* say he was bringing it tonight, Lady Margaret?"

POLLY. "Well, actually, I – I – "

> *(Stops, frowning.)*

GERRY. *Now* what's the matter?

POLLY. I just thought – *Saul* brings the necklace, in the first act, and I put it in the safe – so how can I say – ?

PHYLLIS. *(Offstage.)* Oh, dear! Oh, dear-oh-dear!

> *(Rushes onstage.)*

I forgot to give you the new line! When I rewrote the first act, a few weeks back, I completely forgot about that line in *this* act!

GERRY. This is a hell of a time to think of it! What's the new line?

PHYLLIS. I – I don't have the rewrite *with* me – !

GERRY. *Approximately,* then!

> *(Will get up and move up onto the stage.)*

We don't have time for a lot of fooling around with words! Just give us the *gist* of it and we'll improvise!

PHYLLIS. Well – um – Polly's line is basically the same – only she says something to Billy about him not being here when Saul brought the necklace, instead of Percival, do you see?

GERRY. Can you handle that, Polly?

POLLY. I – I think so – let me try it...

GERRY. Okay. Just get on with this thing!

> *(Starts offstage.)*

I need a cup of coffee. Louise – is there any coffee back there?

LOUISE. *(Offstage.)* For want of a better name.

GERRY. *(Sighs.)* It'll have to do. Come along, Phyllis. The rest of you get back to work!

>   (**GERRY** *and* **PHYLLIS** *exit;* **PLAYERS** *get back in place, and:)*

POLLY. Feed me your line again, Billy – ?

BILLY. Uh...what the hell *is* it? ...Oh, yeah! ... " – He *did* say he was bringing it tonight, Lady Margaret?"

POLLY. "Well, actually, I never spoke with him directly – but there was a message delivered this morning in the post – saying – " uh. " – saying that he'd asked Doctor Forbes to bring it *for* him!"

SMITTY. "What, on Saint Swithin's Day?"

SAUL. Wait a minute, wait a minute! That sounds as if it's against the law to *ask* somebody to *deliver* things on that day – the part about the post has to come last, Polly.

POLLY. Let me try it again... " – but Doctor Forbes told me that Percival had asked *him* to deliver it, in a message delivered this morning in the post!"

SAUL. Ah, much better! Go ahead, Smitty.

SMITTY. "What, on Saint Swithin's Day?"

>   (**SAUL** *guffaws.)*

GERRY. *(Offstage.) Now* what?!

SAUL. I'm sorry. It sounded like she couldn't go *ahead* on –

GERRY. *(Off. Truly angry.)* I don't give a good damn *what* it sounded like! If all you three-year-olds want to play *games* instead of learning this *play* – !

SAUL. *(Much chastened.)* I'm sorry, Gerry. Go on, Smitty, please.

SMITTY. *(Grimly.)* " – Saint Swithin's Day!"

HENRY. "By Jove! Never thought of that! Margaret – are you *certain* about that message?"

POLLY. "Why – come to think of it – no."

VIOLET. "You *didn't* receive a message?"

POLLY. "Oh, yes – I did – but now I wonder if it were actually from Percival!"

BILLY. "But it did come by post?"

POLLY. "I – I assumed it had – but – "

HENRY. "Assumed? You mean, you didn't actually see it?"

POLLY. "Why, no."

> (**PLAYERS** *are now "into rhythm" with their play, and do their roles well until the interruption.*)

VIOLET. "Then how did you know its content?"

POLLY. "Why – Doctor Forbes told me what it had said."

SAUL. "Is there any reason I shouldn't have?"

BILLY. "No, no, of course not, old chap. Only – if there was no delivery of the post, today, then how – ?"

SAUL. "It was not a letter. It was a telegram."

BILLY. "I should like very much to *see* that telegram!"

SAUL. "Well – as a matter of fact – I don't have it. The message was phoned from the telegraph office."

BILLY. "Doris – have there been any telephone messages this evening?"

SAUL. "See here, you insolent young pup! Are you doubting my word?!"

POLLY. "Of course he isn't, Rex! Stephen, you should apologize to Doctor Forbes."

BILLY. "Oh, I shall. As soon as Doris answers my question."

SMITTY. "No, sir."

POLLY. "What, are you quite sure?"

SMITTY. "The telephone has been out of order since this *afternoon,* mum."

BILLY. "Aha! And what do you say to *that*, Doctor Forbes?"

> (*There is a silence;* **PLAYERS** *slowly look toward the silent telephone, waiting; nothing happens; then:*)

LOUISE. *(Offstage.)* Damn it all to hell! Phyllis, what have you done?!

PHYLLIS. *(Offstage.)* What have *I* done? What are you talking about? Did I get the phone bell out of order on the tape?

GERRY. *(Offstage.)* What were *you* doing with the *tape,* Phyllis?!

PHYLLIS. *(Offstage.)* Why – I just thought I'd give a listen to the sound effects and –

LOUISE. *(Offstage.) And you erased the tape!*

> (**PLAYERS** *onstage all slump, and ad-lib mutters of despair.)*

There's *nothing* on it! *Nothing!*

GERRY. *(Offstage.)* Oh, Louise, are you *sure* – ?!

LOUISE. *(Offstage.)* Listen for yourself!

GERRY. *(Offstage.) I* don't hear anything – ?

LOUISE. *(Offstage.)* That's what I *mean!*

> (*From the wings, we hear ad-libs of* **PHYLLIS** *wailing all sorts of apologies,* **GERRY** *trying to make peace,* **AGGIE** *bemoaning the future of the show, and* **LOUISE** *raising hell – all overlapping one another; then* **LOUISE***, with a reel of recording tape, comes onstage, crossing toward far side and the backstage exit.)*

POLLY. Louise! You're not leaving?

LOUISE. *(Stops, center stage.)* Can't do a damn thing for you if I *stay*! I've got to get home and re-tape every one of those sound effects for the opening! *(Shouts offstage.)* And if that bubble-brained idiot so much as comes *near* my machine again, I'm gonna beat her *head* in with it!

> (*She turns to continue her cross, but stops as* **GERRY** *– followed by a weepily contrite* **PHYLLIS** *– hastens onstage.)*

GERRY. Listen – as long as you *have* to do it all over, Louise – I've been thinking – perhaps we should have the telephone *hooked up* – to a button backstage – there are so many phone-calls in this show – wouldn't it be easier to ring the phone manually?

LOUISE. Well...yes, I guess it would – and it'd save me a lot of work tonight if I could leave those rings off the tape –

AGGIE. *(Enters.) I* can do the hookup. The end of the wire's already backstage, and there's a storage battery, too, for power.

LOUISE. *(A bit calmer.)* Okay. Just make sure you put the button somewhere near the tape recorder, so I don't have to leave the sound board to find it.

AGGIE. Of course.

> *(Turns and exits.)*

LOUISE. *Oh,* and the rest of you –

> *(**PLAYERS** turn their attention to her.)*

Remember one thing: When you *use* the phone in the play – be *sure* you hang it *up* right! If it's sitting the wrong way, so the buttons aren't depressed by the speaker part, the phone can't ring, got it?

> *(**PLAYERS** ad-lib assent.)*

Okay. Now if you'll excuse me, I've got a hell of a lot of work to do!

> *(Completes her cross and exits.)*

PHYLLIS. I'm so dreadfully sorry. I feel I owe each and every one of you an apology for what I've done –

GERRY. *(Takes her arm and starts leading her offstage.)* Write it down and *mail* it to them!

> *(As they exit:)*

SAUL. *(Under his breath.)* Preferably on Saint Swithin's Day!

> *(Then all **PLAYERS** react as phone rings.)*

AGGIE. *(Offstage.)* How's *that* for fast work!

GERRY. *(Offstage.)* Beautiful, Aggie, just beautiful! You deserve a cup of coffee for that.

AGGIE. *(Offstage.)* I'll settle for that stuff Louise brews.

SAUL. Shall we go on, or what?

GERRY. *(Offstage.)* Go on, or *else*!

AGGIE. *(Offstage.)* They need their cue.

(*Phone rings.*)

SAUL. "Does *that* answer your question?"

POLLY. "Stephen, I believe you owe Doctor Forbes an apology."

HENRY. *(After a pause.)* Aggie – ?

AGGIE. *(Offstage.)* Oh, sorry! I was drinking my swill!

(*Phone rings again.*)

HENRY. "You had best answer that, Doris, before we owe the *caller* an apology, too!"

SMITTY. *(Moves to phone.)* "Yes, sir!"

(*Answers.*)

"Hello – ? ...Who? ...Why, yes, he is. Just a moment."

(*Hands phone to* **HENRY.**)

"It's for you, sir."

HENRY. "Who is it, Doris?"

SMITTY. "Sir Percival."

SAUL. "It *can't* be – ! ...I mean – "

BILLY. "Yes, Doctor? Exactly what *do* you mean?"

SAUL. "Why – I – I – "

HENRY. *(On phone.)* "Hello? ...What? ...Ah! Yes, I see... Yes, thank you! Thank you very much!"

(*Hangs up.*)

POLLY. "Why – Dudley – you look so strange! What did Percival *say?*"

HENRY. *(Grimly.)* "That was *not* Sir Percival!"

(*Phone rings.*)

What the hell – ?

GERRY. *(Offstage.)* Aggie!

AGGIE. *(Offstage.)* Sorry! I put my coffee cup down on the button!

GERRY. *(Offstage.)* Go on, people, go on!

HENRY. *(Grimly.)* "That was *not* Sir Percival!"

POLLY. "Then – who was it?"

BILLY. "That was Miles Taylor, a good friend of mine."

VIOLET. "Stephen, I do not understand."

POLLY. "Nor I."

BILLY. "It is very simple. I asked Miles to ring up and say he was Sir Percival, so that I could observe the effect it would have upon Doctor Forbes. I think you will all agree that he was struck dumbfounded."

SAUL. "Nonsense!"

HENRY. "It is *not* nonsense, sir! I myself observed the selfsame reaction."

VIOLET. "But – what does it *mean?*"

POLLY. "Yes, what *does* it all mean?"

SMITTY. "Yes, what can it *possibly* mean?"

HENRY. "Doris, you are forgetting your place."

SMITTY. "Sorry, milord."

BILLY. "*I* can explain what it means! It means that this man, after murdering Sir Percival for the necklace – "

SAUL. "How dare you, sir! I'll have you in court for this! Such accusations are actionable! To tarnish my good name – it's libelous!"

BILLY. "I cannot be sued successfully for libel if my accusations should prove true!"

SAUL. *(Sneers.)* "And just how do you *intend* to prove them true?"

BILLY. "Quite easily, after a look at that necklace. Would you mind getting it, Doctor Forbes?"

SAUL. "The necklace? There is no proof on that necklace. I'll show you!"

> *(Steps to safe, dials combination, reaches inside.)*

Aggie!

AGGIE. *(Offstage.)* Oh, golly, I forgot!

(We see her cross doorway, upstage, pass through area upstage of window, pass French doors, during:)

AGGIE. I won't forget tomorrow night! I swear I won't! Things have just been kind of hectic, with Phyllis here, and –

GERRY. *(Steps onstage.)* Aggie, don't cross where the audience can *see* you!

AGGIE. *(Now out of our view near back of safe.)* I won't, I won't. I was just in a hurry!

GERRY. *(Eyes skyward.)* Heaven help us all!

(Exits.)

SAUL. From my line – ?

GERRY. *(Offstage.)* From *anywhere*!

SAUL. "...I'll show you!"

(Reaches arm into safe almost up to the armpit.)

Aggie, can't you stand a little closer?!

AGGIE. *(Offstage.)* Sorry, Saul.

SAUL. *(Hand emerges with necklace.)* "There! Now show me your ridiculous proof!"

BILLY. "You yourself have shown the proof, Doctor Forbes! For – if you are *not* the murderer – how did you know the combination to that *safe*?!"

POLLY. "Great heavens! He's right!"

SAUL. "Blast you, Stephen Sellers!"

(Whips out pistol.)

"But there is one thing you did not take into account! I am armed!"

HENRY. "You, sir, are a scoundrel!"

VIOLET. "And I should very much like to sunder our engagement this moment!"

BILLY. "In that case – will you marry *me*, Diana?"

VIOLET. "With all my heart, Stephen!"

(They do a four-hand clasp and stare adoringly into one another's eyes.)

POLLY. "Doris – telephone at once for the constabulary!"

SAUL. *(Aims pistol.)* "Do so and you are dead, my dear!"

SMITTY. "Oh, mum, what shall I do?"

SAUL. "Just raise your hands. And the rest of you do likewise!"

(All stand there a moment; then:)

Aggie! The telephone's supposed to ring there!

AGGIE. *(Enters through fronch doors.)* I clean forgot! This is going to be *hell* tomorrow night, dashing to the safe with the necklace, then dashing back to ring the phone – not to mention following in the script so I can *cue* people!

PHYLLIS. *(Offstage.)* *I* can pass the necklace to him, tomorrow night, if you like! I'd feel much safer having it in my possession, anyhow.

GERRY. *(Offstage.)* But won't you be seated out front?

PHYLLIS. *(Offstage.)* I can come up for that part – I'll have to be backstage, anyhow, so I can come out for my bow.

GERRY. *(Offstage.)* Well – I don't know...

AGGIE. *(Has finished cross, will exit on:)* We'll hash that out later! Right now, let's get *on* with this thing!

SAUL. Okay! *(Into character.)* "...And the rest of you do likewise!"

(Phone rings.)

"Damn and blast! Who's that?"

BILLY. "It is my friend, Miles Taylor. I told him to ring us back shortly after his first call. If I do not answer – he shall summon the law, and they shall arrive here with a warrant for your arrest – Stanley Grimes!"

POLLY & VIOLET. *(In rhythmic unison.)* "Stanley Grimes?! Do you mean that criminal laboratory assistant to Doctor Forbes?!"

BILLY. "To the *late* Doctor Forbes, unless I miss my guess!"

*(Others – except **SAUL**, of course – gasp.)*

BILLY. "You are done with your fiendish felonies, Grimes. Put down that pistol and surrender!"

SAUL. "Never! I may go to the gallows – but none of you in this room will live to see it!"

SMITTY. *(To **HENRY**.)* "Please, milord – might I leave the room?"

SAUL. "Stand where you are! But – before I destroy you all – I must know – how did you come to suspect me, Sellers?"

BILLY. "I arrived here late, as you all know. As a result, I had time to hear the news broadcast which told of the finding of Sir Percival's body – dead of a rare Indian cobra poison. You, of course, had already disconnected the telephone here at the switchbox, so no one else would hear the news. But when I accidentally knocked down your overcoat as I was hanging up my own – and found a flagon of that very poison in the pocket – why then, I *knew* of course. I immediately reconnected the telephone, rang up Miles, set up our plan, and – "

VIOLET. "Excuse me, my dearest darling, but – *what* did you know when you found this foul fiend's flagon?"

BILLY. "Why, how this man had schemed to keep alive the legend of that curse! He had immersed the necklace in the cobra venom, so that all who handled it would shortly become ill. He thought in that way to devalue it, to make Lady Margaret loathe the sight of it – and then, of course, he could have it for considerably less than its real value, so anxious would she be to sell the bauble!"

POLLY. "And I *would* have been, too! Oh, curse you, Stanley Grimes!"

SAUL. "Curse? Bah! There are no such things as curses! And I have soaked my hands in an antitoxin to prevent penetration of that potent poison, too!"

*(From offstage, we hear **AGGIE** improvising vocally the "Rrrrrr" of a police siren.)*

What the hell is that?!

AGGIE. *(Offstage.)* You get *real* sirens *tomorrow* night!

> (**PLAYERS** *shake their heads, then plow doggedly on.*)

BILLY. "Aha! My delaying tactics have done their work! The law is upon you, Stanley Grimes! Surrender yourself!"

SAUL. "Never! I shall take this necklace, sell it for a fortune, and move wealthily to another country!"

> *(Abruptly staggers, clutches his heart.)*

"Oh! Oh! Oh!"

POLLY. "It's the curse! The curse of the – the – the – " Oh, damn it!

HENRY. "Darjeeling Diamond," dear.

POLLY. Thanks, Henry. "...the curse of the Darjeeling Diamond!"

> (**SAUL** *drops gun, falls "dead";* **HENRY** *rushes to him, takes his pulse, shakes his head.*)

HENRY. "He's dead!"

POLLY. *(Raises forefinger, takes Statue of Liberty stance.)* "Yes. He mocked the laws of society – and now, a higher power has intervened!"

VIOLET. "Oh, Stephen – hold me, hold me!"

> (**BILLY** *embraces her, she pillows her head on his shoulder.*)

AGGIE. *(Offstage.)* Curtain! Shall I lower it, Gerry?

GERRY. *(Coming onstage.)* Hell, no! We're only just begun! Okay, you've *had* your third act! Now – from the top of Act One! It's already half past ten!

SMITTY. My mother is going to *murder* me!

PHYLLIS. *(Steps blithely onstage, smiles brightly, and trills:)* Ah, but my dear, it is in *such* a good *cause*!

> *(And as all others stare at her in disbelief –)*
>
> *(The curtain falls.)*

ACT III

(At curtain rise, we find **PLAYERS** *in curtain call positions, but a bit farther upstage, since* **GERRY** *is standing before them, her back to us.* **PLAYERS** *are garbed as we last saw them, but now* **VIOLET** *wears her wig, and it fits, and all are wearing makeup.)*

(Note: Our real cast has had makeup all along, of course, but now their makeup looks like makeup – too much lip rouge on the men, too much cheek rouge on the women, etc., so that they look like people in a play look to each other in close up – but now we have the benefit of the make believe as well.)

*(***GERRY*** is in a dressy dress, and wearing a corsage.)*

GERRY. Well – this is *it*, gang! Any moment, now, they're going to open the doors and let the audience in.

SMITTY. Do they *have* to?

(Others laugh.)

I'm not sure I'm kidding – I'm really getting scared.

GERRY. That's *good*, Smitty. The worst way to approach a performance is with complacency. Nervousness gives a player energy.

SMITTY. Well, nervousness is giving *this* player creeping *paralysis*! Aggie may have to *push* me onstage!

AGGIE. *(Enters from wings, carrying script.)* And don't think I won't. I used to be a sergeant in the Paratroops. Everybody jumped – whether they wanted to or not.

SAUL. I'm not nervous about the *regular* audience – if we goof, they'll probably never know it – what's giving *me* cold sweat is the thought of looking out front and seeing *Gerry*! She'll recognize every error!

GERRY. Then relax. I won't *be* out front tonight. I'll be right backstage here – helping Aggie push!

POLLY. How come? Don't you *want* to see the show – not that I blame you!

GERRY. Maybe *tomorrow* night. Tonight, *Phyllis* will be out front. If I sit out there, she'll want to be *next* to me – I don't think I could take that.

AGGIE. That reminds me – she still insists on being behind the safe to hand Saul that necklace! It saves me busting my behind galloping from the safe back to help Louise at the sound board – but I'm afraid she may get so wrapped up in listening to her play she may forget!

GERRY. If she does, this play will end with a *real* murder!

(**LOUISE** *enters from backstage door side, carrying tape.*)

LOUISE. Well – I did it. Took me till damn near three o'clock in the morning, but I got all those sounds back in order on the tape, finally!

AGGIE. I hope you skipped the phone bells – ?

LOUISE. Don't worry. But I *did* add thunder and lightning effects.

GERRY. But – why? There's no thunderstorm in this play!

LOUISE. Who ever heard of a murder mystery without a thunderstorm?! Believe me, we're gonna need it.

GERRY. Louise, are you crazy? There's no spot in the play to *have* it!

LOUISE. What do you want to bet?

GERRY. I've been through this play a hundred times – I *know* there's no place to hear a thunderstorm! You'll distract the actors!

LOUISE. Gerry – I guarantee you – there's a *perfect* spot for a thunderstorm effect in this show, and it *won't* distract the actors!

GERRY. Where?!

LOUISE. That's gonna be my surprise.

> *(Others ad-lib "Oh, now, Louise – " or like expostulations.)*

Trust me! Have I ever let you down?

GERRY. But there's *no way* you can –

LOUISE. Make it easy on yourself. Bet me a dollar.

GERRY. *(After a pause.)* You're on!

LOUISE. *(Starts off toward sound board side of stage.)* If there's one thing I love, it's a sucker bet!

> *(Exits.)*

PHYLLIS. *(Offstage.)* *Yoo*-hoo – !

> *(All react.)*

SAUL. That's what I hate about stages – there's no place to hide!

PHYLLIS. *(Enters from stage-door side; she wears an evening gown and a corsage.)* Hel-*lo*, hel-*lo*, hel-*lo*! The magical moment is upon us at last!

GERRY. And so will our audience be, if we don't get this curtain closed!

LOUISE. *(Offstage.)* Will do!

> *(Curtain will close, slowly, during:)*

PHYLLIS. *(Moving hurriedly forward and offstage.)* I just wanted to wish you all the best of luck!

SAUL. In show business, that's bad luck to do! You're supposed to say, "Break a leg!"

PHYLLIS. *(Offstage, and moving toward her seat.)* I'll never understand the theatre.

HENRY. That's a fine thing for our *playwright* to say!

> *(Curtain is now closed, but we can still hear onstage:)*

GERRY. The audience is coming in, now – would you all like to join me in prayer?

VIOLET. I'll say!

BILLY. We could *use* a miracle!

GERRY. Saint Genesius – pray for us!

OTHERS. Saint Genesius – pray for us!

GERRY. Okay, places, everyone – I'm going offstage.

SMITTY. Saul – who's Saint Genesius?

SAUL. The patron saint of actors – he performed for the Roman emperor and they had him put to death.

SMITTY. Oh, boy. I hope there are no emperors out front tonight!

SAUL. Amen!

> *(Music starts; at climax, curtain opens on Act One tableau of* Murder Most Foul *as before.)*

SMITTY. *(Featherdusting safe like crazy.)* "Lord Dudley, will there be anyone at dinner tonight besides Sir Percival the famous archaeologist, Doctor Rex Forbes the famous scientist, and Stephen Sellers the famous millionaire?"

HENRY. "Other than myself and Lady Margaret, my wife, and the lovely socialite Diana Lassiter, here...no, Doris."

SMITTY. *(Starts toward doorway, right.)* "That's what I *thought.*"

> *(Exits, and from offstage, we hear her give a loud:)*

Whew!

HENRY. *(Reacts slightly, then plunges onward.)* "I say, Diana, have you yet located that book on famous jewels of India that I told you must be there on the shelf?"

VIOLET. *(Finding book she has been deliberately overlooking.)* "Ah, yes! Here it is!"

> *(Faces him, flips book open, reacts.)*

"Oh, I say, Lord Dudley – you didn't tell me there was a *curse* on the Ranchipur *Delhi* – I mean the Darjeeling Ruby – *Diamond!*"

HENRY. *(Trying to save her.)* It is known by *many* names, my dear!

VIOLET. It is? ...Oh, yes, it certainly is! Lots of 'em.

HENRY. *(Reverts to his normal line, not realizing it no longer fits, especially as a response to* **VIOLET.***)* "Fiddlesticks! A lot of hogwash!" *(Realizes.)* That *curse*, I mean! ... "Damned superstitious rot!"

> *(**VIOLET**, by now totally "up," just stares at him; he desperately reverse-feeds her line to her.)*

But – doesn't the book distinctly say – ?

VIOLET. *(Home at last.)* Yes! "But the book distinctly says that Lord Clyde Fortescue, the first owner of the – the Darjeeling Diamond! – was found floating in his tub – !" Uh – I don't mean the *diamond* was found floating in his tub!

HENRY. No-no, of course not. But – what *was*? Eh?

VIOLET. *He* was! "In his own blood!"

> *(Stops.)*

HENRY. *(Prompts.)* And the next owner – ?

VIOLET. *(Back on the track.)* "And the next owner, Sir Giles Renfrew, had no sooner purchased the ruby – the diamond – from Lord Clyde's estate, when *he* was found floating in his own stables by his favorite horse! ...*Trampled,* I mean!"

> *(In front row, **PHYLLIS** gives an audible moan; **VIOLET** flashes a frantic look that way, then slogs onward:)*

"And the *next* owner – "

HENRY. *(Forgets he's supposed to interrupt; belatedly remembers.)* "Balderdash! Nonsense! A lot of old wives' tales!"

VIOLET. *(Eliding her line a bit.)* They're all dead, aren't they? ...The owners. Not the old wives.

HENRY. "Yes, but consider: I bought the ruby this morning – and I'm fine!"

(Starts to put hand to his head, realizes and corrects:)

HENRY. "The diamond!"

(Hand to head again, sways.)

VIOLET. "Lord Dudley – is anything wrong?"

PHYLLIS. *(Just audible.)* Everything! Everything!

HENRY. *(As if he hadn't heard – but we can see he had.)* "No-no. Nothing. Just one of my beastly attacks."

VIOLET. *(Jumping ahead two speeches.)* "You don't suppose – ?"

HENRY. *(Determined to get his line in.)* Don't you wonder how long I've been having them?!

VIOLET. Oh! "How long have you had them?"

HENRY. "Since this morning."

VIOLET. *(Totally lost improvises.)* That long, huh?

HENRY. *(Controlling his rage.)* Do you suppose that I suppose – ?!

VIOLET. "You don't suppose – ?"

HENRY. "Ridiculous! Sheer coincidence! Merest chance!"

*(**SMITTY** bolts onstage, and since their panic is contagious:)*

SMITTY. Doctor Dud is here, Lord Forbley!

HENRY. *(Staggered, inflects as though naming the fiancé:)* "Ah! It is your fiancé *Diana!*"

*(Both **WOMEN** stare at him.)*

" – your *fiancé*, Diana!"

*(**PHYLLIS** sighs audibly.)*

VIOLET. "Yes, being engaged to the world-famous scientist has made me the envy of all the girls in London – in *England* – in *London, England*!"

HENRY. *("Up.")* Uh.

SMITTY. *(After a moment, tries to help by saying his line.)* "Ah, but a lovely belle like you deserves to be rung!" *(Thinks.)* " – to have a ring!"

VIOLET. *(To* SMITTY, *naturally.)* "You flatter me, Lord Dudley."

HENRY. Uh.

AGGIE. *(Off. Giving him his line, in a hoarse whisper.)* "Doris-will-you-show-the-gentleman-in"!

SMITTY. *(Before he can even echo the cue.)* "At once, milord!"

> *(She exits; no one enters.)*

AGGIE. *(Offstage.)* Saul!

SAUL. *(Offstage.)* Coming!

> *(Dashes onstage, gives clumsy bow.)*

"Lord Dudley. Diana."

HENRY. "I'm sure you young people will want to be alone. I'll just toddle off to my room and putter about."

> *(As in earlier error, moves to upstage doorway, starts to exit right, but stops as we all hear:)*

GERRY. *(Offstage.)* You're going the wrong way!

HENRY. Oh!

> *(Turns full about and exits left, instead, so that we see him passing upstage of the window as he goes.)*

SAUL. *(Who has seen this of course.)* He – he must be going to use the *outside* stairway!

VIOLET. *(Likewise.)* Yes. That must be it. *(Pause.)* Well –

SAUL. *(Galvanized back into character, shouts window ward:)* "Really, Lord Dudley, you needn't go."

HENRY. *(From in back of garden backdrop, where he is working his way toward stage right wings – and will wobble the upstage corridor wall in the process.)* "Nonsense. I was once in love, myself!"

> *(We hear him stumble and fall.)*

Damn it!

SAUL. *(Rushes to* VIOLET, *quickly.)* "My dearest darling!"

VIOLET. "My sweet!"

(They kiss lightly, then stand apart.)

SAUL. "My darling, I have a little surprise – "

(Starts frantically feeling his empty pockets.)

PHYLLIS. Oh, dear!

(Jumps up, exits up aisle, and while she is making her way to the backstage area, our duo ad-libs desperately:)

VIOLET. I like surprises.

SAUL. I kinda thought you did.

VIOLET. I can't wait to find out what it is.

SAUL. It's really worth waiting for.

VIOLET. I'm so excited.

SAUL. I knew you would be.

VIOLET. Can't find it, huh?

SAUL. *(Inspired.) I* know! I must have left it in my coat! Excuse me!

(Rushes out right doorway; **VIOLET**, *nothing to do and nobody to talk to, stands awhile swinging her arms back and forth, and whistling, all the while we hear:)*

The necklace! Where the hell's the necklace?!

AGGIE. *(Offstage.)* Phyllis has it! I forgot to get it from her!

(We hear footsteps, and:)

PHYLLIS. *(Offstage.)* Here it is! I'm so terribly sorry!

SAUL. *(Offstage.)* Just give it to me!

(Rushes onstage, then realizes he holds:)

PHYLLIS. *(Offstage.)* My evening bag!

SAUL. *(To* **VIOLET**.*)* Whoops! Wrong surprise!

(Dashes off, and we hear:)

I hope you're satisfied! *Now* they think Doctor Forbes is a *sissy*!

(Dashes back on with necklace, waves it wearily.)

Surprise! " – the White Ruby of Ranchipur!" Or *whatever* it is!

VIOLET. "Oh! How incredibly lovely it is! Might I – try it on?"

SAUL. *(Slowly sliding into character.)* "Not afraid of the curse?"

VIOLET. "Well – not *very* much... May I – please – ?"

SAUL. "Certainly you shall. Here, allow me..."

> *(She turns, he hangs it about her neck, but does not quite get the catch in place, and it slides right out of sight into the bosom of her dress as he turns her around to face him and says his line "on automatic":)*

"It *is* lovely – in such a lovely *setting*!"

> *(Realizes he can't see it; without thinking, leans forward to peer down into her cleavage;* **VIOLET** *slaps both palms to the area and turns desperately away.)*

VIOLET. "Oh, Rex, what a thing to say – !"

SAUL. *(Staring at the back of her head.)* "I cannot decide which is lovelier, you or that fabulous gem."

> *(***PHYLLIS*** *will come down the aisle and regain her seat, tiptoeing so as not to disturb anyone, during:)*

VIOLET. *(Both hands frantically groping in her cleavage.)* "I simply – must see – myself in it – let me – go find a mirror!"

> *(Starts toward right doorway, still groping, but stops and drops her hands as* **POLLY** *enters.)*

POLLY. "Diana! That necklace – !"

> *(Doesn't see it, and doesn't know where it is, either.)*

Where *is* it?

VIOLET. *(Points demurely into depths of her cleavage.)* In here.

POLLY. *(Dazed, but dogged.)* "How dare you! Take it out at once! ... – *off* at once!"

SAUL. *(Desperately trying to get necklace, while* **VIOLET** *just as desperately tries to keep his hands off her.)* I'll get it!

POLLY. *(Improvising.)* Well, hurry it up!

VIOLET. *(Gets necklace out with an effort, extends it to* **POLLY**.*)* There! "Lady Margaret! I was only – "

POLLY. "Take it off, I say! This instant!"

SAUL. *(Grabs it from* **VIOLET**.*)* "Here, now, Lady Margaret, there's surely no harm done...?"

> *(***PHYLLIS*** *gives an audible moan.)*

> *(Note: This next bit is tricky, so pay attention: We must indicate that first act get finished, but we of course do not have time to do an entire play in this remaining act, so here is how it is accomplished: From here on, dialogue is pre-taped and will be lip-synced by* **PLAYERS** *– at double speed – simultaneous with a strobe-light being used to illustrate stage, so that the* **PLAYER***'s sped-up movements will look even jerkier – and – at the indicated spot – the curtain will close, even though the action and dialogue continues. Ready? Here goes:)*

POLLY. "No harm, you say? How could you endanger the life of this dear girl – and your own fiancée!"

VIOLET. "Oh, I don't believe in that silly curse, Lady Margaret! After all, this *is* the twentieth century!"

> *(Places back of hand to forehead, sways.)*

SAUL. "Diana! Are you all right?"

> *(Curtain starts to close, slowly.)*

VIOLET. *(The volume of pre-taped speech will dwindle, fast, to total silence, during her line:)* "Yes – yes, I think so.

It was just momentary – the room seemed to dip – my head started to spin..."

(In the silence, we hear:)

AGGIE. *(Offstage.)* Places for Act Two, everybody!

*(Music starts, and curtain opens on **VIOLET**, seated on sofa; **BILLY** enters as music fades; pace and voices are "live" and normal, now.)*

BILLY. "Oh! Diana. I was seeking Lady Margaret."

VIOLET. "Lady Margaret is cutting roses in the garden, Stephen."

(Demurely folds hands in lap.)

"She – may not return for some time."

BILLY. "Would you mind if I waited for her...here?"

VIOLET. "Naturally not."

BILLY. "Might I...sit?"

(Goes to step forward from doorway – and his coat is snagged on frame [i.e.: someone backstage holds onto end of it till his release] – and he ends up leaning forward and swaying like a loose ship's figurehead.)

VIOLET. *(With eyes demurely downcast, has not seen.)* "If you are so *inclined*!"

(Looks up, sees him, gapes.)

BILLY. *(Abruptly frees coat [let it go, here] lurches sofaward, sprawls across right arm of sofa and lands with his face in **VIOLET**'s lap; he raises his head for:)* "Diana – "

VIOLET. "Yes, Stephen – ?"

BILLY. "Would you take offense if I were to – to – ?"

VIOLET. "Stephen, what are you trying to say?"

BILLY. *(Will squirm into sitting position beside her, during:)* "Oh, dash it all, Diana, must we play at words?! You *know* the message that longs to cry out from within my heart!"

VIOLET. "Is it possible – do I dare for a moment imagine – that the message in your heart is the selfsame message that cries out from within my own?"

> *(Then she looks down, reacts to what she sees, and – if delivering that message – whispers hoarsely:)*

Your *fly* is open!

BILLY. *(Frantically claps both hands onto his lap, and in his panic jumps two speeches ahead.)* "And yet – you do not draw away...?"

> *(Once more, we go to pre-tape speed-up, strobe, and slow curtain, during:)*

VIOLET. "Oh, Stephen – can you not reason out *why*?!"

BILLY. "I – I am almost afraid to!"

VIOLET. "Then *cease* your noble trepidations, Stephen Sellers. For – though I am a high-born lady – I am also a woman!"

BILLY. "Oh, Diana!"

> *(Kisses her lightly – and fast, with the speed-up – on the lips.)*

VIOLET. "Oh, Stephen!"

> *(They kiss again, and the curtain is closed, now as we hear an accelerating speed-up alternation of "Oh-Diana-Oh-Stephen-Oh-Diana-Oh-Stephen-[etc.]" until the pitch is higher than bats or dogs could hear it, and then music starts, and we hear:)*

AGGIE. *(Off. Normal speed and voice.)* Everybody ready for Act Three! Places! Places!

GERRY. *(Offstage.)* You know, Aggie, maybe I *should* have gone to that bar, after all!

AGGIE. *(Offstage.)* If you change your mind, I'll *join* you! The Paratroops was never like *this*!

LOUISE. *(Offstage.)* You know the difference between a play and a parachute?

AGGIE. *(Off. Warily.)* What, Louise?

LOUISE. *(Offstage.)* When a *parachute* opens, you have nothing to *worry* about!

> *(**AGGIE** and **GERRY** groan.)*

GERRY. *(Offstage.)* Oh, open the damned curtain!

> *(Curtain opens as music stops, on final act tableau.)*

VIOLET. "Ah, Lord Dudley, you give the most charming parties in the whole of England!"

HENRY. "You are too kind, Diana. A pity Sir Percival could not be here."

POLLY. "Do you know – I'm *worried* about Percival! He's never accepted an invitation to one of our parties and then not shown up – at least, not without sending word."

BILLY. "Ah, but Lady Margaret, he might have had motor trouble."

VIOLET. "Yes, indeed. I do hope *he* hasn't had – " Uh. " – I do hope he *hasn't* had – hasn't *had* – had an *accident*!"

> *(Other **PLAYERS**, who had tensed during her struggle, now relax, and are taken unawares by her Freudian slip:)*

"These words can be treacherous at night...*roads*!"

POLLY. "Don't say such a thing! It would make one think that perhaps there was some truth, after all, in that story about the curse!"

HENRY. "Nonsense, my dear. There's no such thurng as a keest – king as a thirst – *thing-as-a-curse*!"

BILLY. "And yet – everyone who has ever owned the – Darjeeling Diamond – has always met with a deadful dremise!"

> *(**PHYLLIS** gives an angry grunt of frustration.)*

VIOLET. *(Determined not to make an error again.)* "But Percival doesn't own the *di*-a-mond anymore – not since he sold it to Lord Dudley for Lady Margaret's col-*lec*-tion."

(Sinks back in armchair with sigh of relief.)

SAUL. "Nevertheless – "

(It is slightly "neverthelesh," and he is over-enunciating just enough so that our suspicions match those of:)

GERRY. *(Offstage.)* Has Saul been taking a nip between acts?!

LOUISE. *(Offstage.)* Wouldn't *you*?

SAUL. *(Has taken a dramatic pause, now continues:)* " – Percival *did* own it – and that mi' be uh-nuff!"

(Smiles dopily and sways ever-so-slightly.)

BILLY. "See here, Doctor Forbes – you are a man of science – soorly *you* don't believe in curshes?"

AGGIE. *(Offstage.)* Louise! Has *Billy* – ?

LOUISE. *(Offstage.)* Saul hates to drink alone.

GERRY. *(Offstage.)* Oh, dear God!

SAUL. "I only know there are strange things in the hishry of Inja – things which defy rashnul esplanation."

*(Note: At no time will **SAUL** or **BILLY** actually stagger, stumble, or sway beyond the merest slight rocking-in-place; they are not falling down drunk; they merely find the world a warm, funny and fuzzy place to be, and are pleased by this sensation.)*

HENRY. "Nonsense. Sheer cockycock. Superstitious dribble!"

SAUL. "Quite posply, Lordudley – an' yet – "

POLLY. "And yet – ?"

SAUL. *(Holds up a finger as if to speak, then peers around the room a second, then says with deep significance:)* "*Where* is Sir Percival?"

VIOLET. "Frankly, I'm *glad* he's not here!"

POLLY. "Why, Diana, what a thing to say!"

SAUL. Yes, indeedy!

BILLY. I'll say!

> (*Both smile inanely at one another.*)

VIOLET. (*A little staggered by their improvisations.*) "I mean it. Sir Percival is – no gentleman."

HENRY. "Here, now, what are you saying?"

VIOLET. (*Obviously with her mind elsewhere than on her line.*) "When he looks at me – I feel as though my hands were moving all over his body."

PHYLLIS. (*Just audible.*) Oh, dear. Oh, dear-oh-dear!

POLLY. (*Has almost laughed at* **VIOLET***'s line, but manages to force her line out amid near-convulsive twitches from the mirth bubbling up and trying to escape her lips.*) "But he is a knight of the *prrzztt*!"

> (*This last is a laugh raspberrying through pursed lips.*)

VIOLET. (*At sea, since she didn't hear her own line at all.*) "He is a disgusting toad. And such toads can be lecherous at night!"

> (**SMITTY** *hastens onstage on cue, but must wait her line for:*)

SAUL. Yes, indeedy!

BILLY. I'll say!

> (*Same smile business at one another.*)

SMITTY. (*Slightly shaken.*) "Begging your pardon, milord, but should we delay dinner any? Longer?"

HENRY. "Mmm – no, I think not. Can't wait for Percival forever."

> (*Moves toward* **POLLY**.)

"Shall we, my dear?"

POLLY. "I suppose so. But – don't you think someone should call Percival's flat and ascertain the reason for his absence?"

BILLY. *(Moves around* **VIOLET***'s chair to take her arm as she rises, but* she *takes* his *arm to steady him.)* "Do you know – that might be a sound idea. There is something distinctly odd about all of this."

VIOLET. "All of what, Stephen?"

BILLY. "This business about Percival and the neckulace. *Neck*ulace. He *did* say he was bringing it tonight, Lady Margaret?"

POLLY. "Well, actually, I never spoke with him directly – but there was a message delivered this morning on the post – *in* the post – *on* the post – the *mailman* brought it!"

SMITTY. *(Fuddled by the reworded cue.)* "What, on Swithin's Day? ...*Saint* Swithin's! ...*Day!*"

HENRY. "By Jove! Never thought of that! Margaret – are you *certain* about that – uh – that mailman – or whatever you said."

POLLY. "Why – come to think of it – no."

VIOLET. *(Trying to follow the alterations.)* "You *didn't* receive a mailman?"

POLLY. Message!

VIOLET. That, too.

POLLY. "Oh, yes – I did – but now I wonder if it were actually from Percival!"

BILLY. "But it did come on a post?"

POLLY. "I – I assumed it had – but – "

HENRY. "Assumed? You mean, you didn't actually see it – him – the message *or* the mailman?"

POLLY. *Whatever* it was – *no*!

VIOLET. "Then how do you know its *content*?"

POLLY. "Why – Doctor Forbes told me what it had said."

SAUL. Yes, indeedy!

BILLY. *(The soberer of the two, sees that* **SAUL** *is not about to give him his cue, so reverses his line to his own:)* Is there any *reason* why you *shouldn't* have?

SAUL. *(Altered.)* "Is there any reason I shouldn't have?"

BILLY. "No, no, of course not, old chap. Only – "

SAUL. *(Interrupts.)* Then why'd you *ask*?

BILLY. *(Getting a grip on himself.)* "On-ly...if there was no delivery of the post, today, then how – "

SAUL. "It was not a letter. It was a telephone. Cable car. *Telegram!*"

> *(Aware of his own inadequacies for the first time, he is starting to regain some control.)*

BILLY. "I should like very much to *see* that telegram!"

SAUL. *(Starts searching pockets, takes out pistol, shakes his head, replaces pistol, then remembers:)* Hey! I haven't got it! ...uh... "As a matter of fact. The message was phoned from the telegraph office."

BILLY. "Doris – have there been any telephone messages this evening?"

SAUL. "See here, you innocent young punk! Are you doubting my word?!"

POLLY. "Of course he isn't, Rex! ..."

> *(Goes "up.")*

"Of course he isn't, Rex..."

AGGIE. *(Off. Cuing with next word.)* "Stephen – "

POLLY. *(Thinking she's flubbed the name.)* "Of course he isn't, Stephen!"

BILLY. *(Helpfully.)* Should I apologize to Doctor Forbes?

POLLY. *(Sincerely.)* Yes, thank you!

BILLY. "Oh, I shall. As soon as – as – "

SMITTY. I'm *Doris.*

BILLY. " – Doris answers my question."

SMITTY. *(Got lost while helping.)* ...What was the question?

> **(PLAYERS** *all look desperately at one another.)*

POLLY. *Someone* must remember!

SAUL. *(Almost sober, now, but just as lost as the rest.)* Damned if *I* do!

VIOLET. Me, neither!

HENRY. Doesn't *anyone* know?

SMITTY. *(Suddenly remembers her line.)* "No, sir!"

BILLY. No, *what*?

SMITTY. That's the answer to the *question*!

POLLY. *(Without thinking, says the right line by accident:)* "What, are you quite sure?"

SMITTY. "The telephone has been out of order since this afternoon: *Mum!*"

BILLY. "Aha! And what do you say to *that*, Doctor Forbes?"

> *(Silence;* **PLAYERS** *covertly look toward phone, and we hear galloping footsteps backstage, and:)*

AGGIE. *(Offstage.)* Oh, damn it!

> *(Phone rings.)*

SAUL. "Does *that* answer your question?"

POLLY. "Stephen, I believe you owe Doctor Forbes an apology."

> *(Phone rings again.)*

HENRY. "You had best answer that, Doris..."

SMITTY. *(Hesitates, reverse-feeds him his incompleted line.)* Before we owe the *caller* an apology, too?

HENRY. *(Anything to get to the final curtain.)* Yes, damn it, yes!

SMITTY. *(Leaps to phone.)* Yes, sir, you bet!

> *(Grabs it up, and in her anxiety forgets to pause for the supposed caller's part of the dialogue with her.)*

"Hello? Who? Why, yes, he is. Just a moment."

> *(Thrusts phone at* **HENRY.***)*

It's for you.

> *(Starts away, turns swiftly back.)*

Sir!

> *(Moves away.)*

HENRY. *(Flustered, forgets his line to* **SMITTY**, *speaks right on phone.)* "Hello? ...What? ..."

> *(Then remembers, goes wide-eyed, shouts after* **SMITTY**.)

"Who is it, Doris?"

SMITTY. "Sir Percival."

> *(Before* **SAUL** *can say his line, a confused* **HENRY** *gets right back on phone, with:)*

HENRY. "Ah! Yes, I see... Yes, thank you! Thank you very much!"

SAUL. *(Better late than never.)* "It *can't* be! ...I mean – "

HENRY. *(So shaken, he sets phone down on stand beside cradle.)* You mean it can't be *Sir Percival*, right?

SAUL. Uh. Right!

BILLY. *(Dismally plunges into his own line.)* "Yes, Doctor? Exactly what *do* you mean?"

SAUL. "Why – I – I – "

> *(***PLAYERS** *look at* **HENRY**, *since it is now he is supposed to go to the phone, but of course he's already been there.)*

HENRY. Uh – I'm *off* the phone, Polly – *Margaret*!

POLLY. Off the – ? But – ? Oh! "Why-Dudley-you-look-so-strange-what-did-Percival-say?"

HENRY. *(Relieved to be back on the track.)* "That was *not* Sir Percival!"

POLLY. "Then – who was it?"

BILLY. *(Calmly.)* "That was – " *(Less calmly.)* " – uh – a good friend of mine..." *(Sincerely.)* I can't quite remember his name!

SAUL. *(Helpfully.)* Miles Taylor!

BILLY. Right!

VIOLET. "Stephen, I do not understand."

POLLY. "Nor I."

BILLY. *(Still panicky, skips eight speeches.)* "I can explain what it means! It means that this man, after murdering Sir Percival for the necklace – " *(Half-realizes.)* Did – did I say he was struck dumfounded?

HENRY. *(Trying to help, but just as lost.)* "I saw – observed – the selfsame reaction – I think."

SMITTY. *(When other **WOMEN** stand there, lost, skips their lines.)* "Yes, what can it *possibly* mean?"

HENRY. *(Joyful to recognize a cue, jumps in:)* "Doris, you are forgetting your place!"

AGGIE. *(Offstage.)* She's not the *only* one!

GERRY. *(Offstage.)* Where the hell *are* they?

AGGIE. *(Offstage.)* Search *me!*

> (**PLAYERS** *have heard, and reacted, and look very forlorn to realize they're unlikely to be prompted.*)

HENRY. *(For want of something better, repeats.)* "Doris, you are forgetting your place!"

SAUL. *(The scene seems familiar, so he comes in, not realizing he's skipped **BILLY***'s accusation, so that it now sounds as if he's chiding **HENRY**.)* "How dare you, sir! I'll have you in court for this! Such accusations are actionable! To tarnish my good name – it's libelous!"

PHYLLIS. *(Jumps to her feet.)* Oh! Oh, dear!

> (*Turns and rushes frantically up aisle to get backstage.*)

BILLY. *(Has paused and squinted out into theatre to seek the source of the disturbance, gives it up, and:)* "I cannot be sued successfully for libel if my accusations should prove true!"

SAUL. *(Sneers.)* "And just how do you *intend* to prove them true?"

BILLY. "Quite easily, after a look at that necklace. Would you mind getting it, Doctor Forbes – ?"

SAUL. "The necklace? There is no proof on that necklace. I'll show you!"

> *(Goes to safe, dials combination, reaches inside – and his face goes ghastly when he finds nothing.)*

Uh – I'm *sure* it's in here *someplace*! …

> *(Removes his hand from safe, and we can hear – but he doesn't – footfalls backstage as* **PHYLLIS** *arrives.)*

Are – are you sure that's where you put it – Margaret – ?

POLLY. *(Not much good at ad-libbing, does a large shrug.)* Like, where *else*?!

BILLY. Uh – why don't you have another look?

SAUL. Oh, all right!

> *(Turns, opens half-closed safe door – and out comes* **PHYLLIS**'s *hand, holding the necklace, to the elbow; he slumps, but takes it, waits till her hand is withdrawn, then slams safe door and turns.)*

"There! Now show me your ridiculous proof!"

BILLY. "You yourself have shown the proof, Doctor Forbes! For – if you are *not* the murderer – how did you know the combination to that *safe*?!"

POLLY. "Great heavens! He's right!"

SAUL. "Blast you, Stephen Sellers!"

> *(Tries to whip out pistol – it is snagged in his pocket.)*

"But there – there is one thing – you did not – did not take into account – !"

> *(And with a ripping noise, pistol comes out, half a pocket lining dangling from the barrel.)*

"I am armed!"

HENRY. "You, sir, are a scoundrel!"

VIOLET. "And I should very much like to sunder our engagement this moment!"

BILLY. "In that case – will you marry *me*, Violet?"

VIOLET. *(Overjoyed.)* Oh, Billy!

    (Flings her arms around him.)

BILLY. *(Terrified.)* I mean *"Diana"*!

VIOLET. *(Releases him.)* Oh, darn!

    (Remembers it's her line, grabs his hands.)

"With all my heart, Stephen!"

POLLY. "Doris – telephone at once for the constabulary!"

SAUL. *(Finally manages to get pocket lining off pistol.)* "Do so and you are dead, my dear!"

SMITTY. "Oh, mum, what shall I do?"

SAUL. "Just raise your hands. And the rest of you do likewise!"

    (PHYLLIS *will come down aisle and regain her seat, during:)*

HENRY. *(Wondering why the phone didn't ring, but not looking at it.)* Did you say – *(Loudly, toward* **AGGIE** *backstage.)* "And the rest of you do likewise!"?

AGGIE. *(Off. Hoarse whisper.)* Hang up the phone!

    (HENRY *looks blankly into his empty palm, dazed.)*

GERRY & AGGIE. *(Off. A bit louder than a whisper.)* Hang up the phone!

    (All **PLAYERS** *save* **SAUL** *– since they are all facing away from the phone – now look similarly into their empty palms, just as dazed as* **HENRY;** **SAUL** *suddenly sees, beyond them, what the problem is, and finds himself in a trio, on:)*

SAUL, GERRY & AGGIE. *(Off. A very audible shout.)* Hang up the phone!

(**SMITTY** *turns, quickly hangs it up, and no sooner is receiver back into cradle than phone rings.*)

SAUL. "Damn and blast! Who's that?!"

BILLY. "It is my friend, Miles Taylor. I told him to ring us back shortly after his first call. If I do not answer – he shall summon the law, and they shall arrive here with a warrant for your arrest – Stanley Grimes!"

> (*Note: We are about to "cheat" a bit; your audience has already heard the finale-to-the-inner-play in its entirety, but unless they have memories like a computer, they won't notice that we are about to shorten that ending quite a bit, to get to the real ending of the real show. So here is how the inner-play-finish goes from here on:*)

POLLY & VIOLET. "Stanley Grimes!"

BILLY. "So put down that pistol and surrender!"

SAUL. "Never! I shall take this necklace, sell it for a fortune, and move wealthily to another country!"

> (*We hear police sirens nearing, outside French doors.*)

POLLY. "Oh, curse you, Stanley Grimes!"

SAUL. (*Clutches his heart.*) "Oh! Oh! Oh!"

POLLY. "It's the curse! The curse of the Delhi Diamond!"

VIOLET. Ranchipur Diamond!

BILLY. Darjeeling Diamond!

HENRY. (*Disgusted with the whole thing.*) *All* of them!

> (*Moves to* **SAUL**, *lifts his wrist, but* **SAUL** *has not dropped the gun this time, and it fires;* **HENRY** *jumps a foot away.*)

POLLY. (*Who has raised her forefinger to say her actual line, has reacted at the same time, and instead says:*) What the hell was that?!

(Curtain closes swiftly, music comes up, and
PHYLLIS *jumps to her feet, applauding.)*

PHYLLIS. Author! Author!

(Curtains open, and we see frazzled players
not quite in curtain call position, but they
quickly get into it and start bowing [with
PHYLLIS *leading applause, your audience*
should be applauding, now, too], then gesture
wingward, and **GERRY** *comes smilingly*
onstage to center, taking a bow herself, and
then all gesture to **PHYLLIS,** *who gaily trots to*
stage, and gets up on it, and **GERRY** *graciously*
moves back to end of lined up **PLAYERS** *to*
allow **PHYLLIS** *center stage – and* **PHYLLIS**
reaches into her evening bag, takes out a
folded sheaf of paper, opens it, and holds out
her hands to "shush" applause, then holds
paper before her, clears her throat, and:)

PHYLLIS. *(Reading from paper.)* My dear friends and fellow
theatre lovers – I cannot thank you enough for the
warm reception you have given my modest effort here
tonight – but I *would* like to take this opportunity to
discuss with you the state of the theatre in America
today –

*(***PLAYERS** *and* **GERRY** *are looking at her,*
aghast, and then all smile as **PHYLLIS** *– her*
lips still moving in unheard speech – is
quite drowned out by violent thunderstorm
sound effects [the crackle-bam-crackle-boom-
crackle-blam sort that goes on without any
silent intervals]; after a moment, **PHYLLIS***'s*
lips stop moving, and she looks up and about
and around in bewilderment – as **LOUISE**
steps just fractionally onstage, and extends
her hand, and **GERRY** *is already moving to*
her with a dollar bill, which she places in
her hand, and **LOUISE** *smiles, pocketing it,*

and **PLAYERS** *laugh in merriment and hang onto each other with the giddiness of their glee, and* **PHYLLIS** *jams her fists against her hips, her face twisted in chagrin, and – as thunderstorm continues unabated – .)*

(The curtain falls.)

(Note: Waste no time here in doing your real curtain call, opening curtain – over music – to an empty stage, and having all **PLAYERS** *(remember, this includes* **AGGIE**, **GERRY**, **LOUISE**, *and* **PHYLLIS**, *now) come out from opposite sides in pairs – one from right doorway, one from French doors – meet at center, bow, spread apart so next couple can enter and do same, etc., till all ten stalwarts have earned their real kudos from your audience.)*

PROPERTY LIST

ACT I
Preset: folding metal chairs in sofa/armchair areas
Players: scripts (manuscript size); cups of coffee
Louise: roll of gaffer's tape
Aggie: script; empty tray for coffee cups
Gerry: cup of coffee; second cup of coffee

ACT II
Preset: sofa and armchair (and, if you exercised option, window drapes, books, liquor tray); upstage corridor wall
Clear: folding chairs, scripts
Gerry: script, yellow pad and pencil, for entrance
Violet: oversize wig to carry onstage
Louise: necklace; reel of recording tape
Smitty: feather duster
Aggie: necklace (from Louise); necklace (from its fall in back of safe), and subsequent cross in view upstage of window; non-physical: must make "Rrrrr" imitation of police siren at appropriate spot
Saul: pistol in pocket

ACT III
Players: heightened makeup to *look* like makeup
Aggie: script
Louise: reel of recording tape for entrance
Phyllis: evening bag with necklace and speech in it: necklace to thrust out through open safe door
Smitty: feather duster
Saul: pistol in pocket; already torn pocket lining in pocket to bring out on barrel of pistol; evening bag; necklace
Gerry: dollar to give Louise just before curtain

SOUND EFFECTS

(listed in order they occur in each act)

ACT I

HAMMERING offstage

HAMMERING and CLUNK of dropped hammer

CRASH of dropped crockery

PHONE BELL

offstage DOOR SLAM for Phyllis's exit

PHONE BELL twice; musical AUTO-HORN, GUNSHOT, AUTO-HORN, GUNSHOT, SCREECH OF TIRES

uninterrupted succession of AUTO-HORN, THUNDERING FOOTSTEPS, SCREECH OF TIRES, GUNSHOT-SCREAM-GUNSHOT-SCREAM (etc. to curtain)

ACT II

CLATTER of necklace falling beyond safe

series of five PHONE BELLS (interspersed with dialogue)

ACT III

Henry's STUMBLE FALL upstage of wall flat

two pre-taped-dialogue-speed-ups

Aggie's GALLOPING FOOTSTEPS prior to her ringing PHONE BELL

next PHONE BELL

Phyllis's FOOTFALLS backstage as she rushes to safe with necklace

Saul's POCKET-RIP

final PHONE BELL

ferocious THUNDERSTORM SOUNDS

RECOMMENDATIONS

1. Sexes of Players: Though *Murder Most Foul* cast, and Phyllis, must remain as indicated, Gerry, Louise, and Aggie can be played by males, if that's simpler for you. Respectively, they can be "Jerry" (whom Phyllis calls "Jerome," and whose husband Frank becomes wife "Frances"), "Louie," and "Algie" (whom Phyllis calls "Algernon").

2. For each act, house lights will darken totally when act starts; but in Act Two, dim house lights only *halfway*, so your audience will know act is starting, then the *rest of the way* when it is indicated that the house lights supposedly darken for first time.

3. If duplicate wigs for Violet are a problem, then simply have her use a single wig, but in Act Two place it well forward on her brow when she dons it, to justify her subsequent lines, then in normal position for Act Three.

4. Music. You will need *two* sets of atmospheric music, a bright and cheery upbeat number for the *real* play, and a moody (and *brief*) number – mysterious and dark, ending on an ominous chord – for curtains of *Murder Most Foul* within the real play. This is very important, in order to cue your audience as to which play-act they are about to see, at any given time. It also gives you a guarantee that they'll know the within-the-play curtain-call from the real curtain-call. In this way, your cast can accept its due from the audience *twice*! (It's dirty pool, but so what?)

5. That Act Three Chaos. Feel free to add any additional slip-ups in *Murder Most Foul* that you wish, in the final act. (Sad to say, you will find them whether you want to or not, during your rehearsals of *PLAY ON!*) There are many "spot goofs" to be added, such as having Violet's curse-book an overlarge tome with a visible title in Act Two, so that she can read it "upside down" when the moment arrives in Act Three, to your audience's delight – or, if possible – let her "pad" her oversized wig with a slightly inflated balloon for Act Three, one from which the air can slowly escape, so that she will be that "British sheepdog" by the end of the show. Etcetera. The more horrible the slips, and the more desperate the cast, in your final act, the funnier the show.

6. Morale-booster. Although this play is somewhat tricky to do, with those varying repeats of the same inner-play scenes – keep this in mind: if somebody *does* goof, and has to be prompted – the audience will never know the difference, and simply think it's part of the show as initially designed. It is *best*, of course, if you do only the slip-ups outlined in this script – but if you really goof – be of good cheer: No one will know.

7. Very special recommendation. Much as your author prides himself on his comedic expertise, he found himself topped, hilariously, in southern California, when the Garden Grove Community Players surprised him (while he was in unsuspecting attendance) with a

killingly funny variation on the final tableau of the show. To achieve this superlative effect yourself: On page 75 of the script, right after Gerry says "You're on!", have all the *other* players ad-lib the likes of "*I'd* like a piece of that!", "Me, too!" etc., and follow their overlapping enthusiasms, of course, with Louise's scripted exit line "If there's one thing I love, it's a sucker bet!" Then let the play proceed as written *until* that final tableau (with Phyllis vainly trying to be heard over the thunderstorm), at which time Louise – with a quietly triumphant smile – strolls along the already-in-a-row group of Gerry and Players, with her hand out palm-upward, and *each of them in turn* (with a grin of rueful amusement) produces and deposits a dollar into Louise's waiting palm. The audience-laughter will be all but deafening.

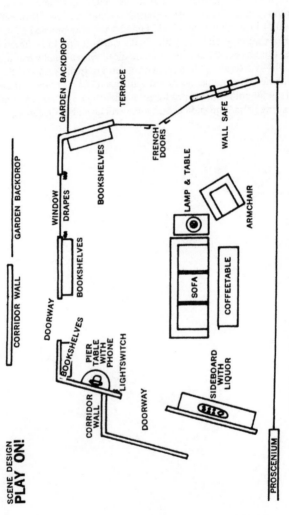

SCENE DESIGN
PLAY ON!

9 780573 613616